D0875348

THE BLACK HERALDS

THE BLACK HERALDS

BY

CESAR VALLEJO

TRANSLATED

BY

RICHARD SCHAAF

AND

KATHLEEN ROSS

UNIVERSITY OF NEW BRUNSWICK

OCT 7 1991

LIBRARIES

LATIN AMERICAN LITERARY REVIEW PRESS
SERIES: DISCOVERIES
PITTSBURGH, PENNSYLVANIA

YVETTE E. MILLER, EDITOR

1990

The Latin American Literary Review Press publishes Latin American creative writing under the series title *Discoveries*, and critical works under the series title *Explorations*.

No part of this book may be reproduced by any means, including information storage and retrieval or photocopying except for short excerpts quoted in critical articles, without the written permission of the publisher.

Translation © 1990 Latin American Literary Review Press

Library of Congress Cataloging-in-Publication Data

Vallejo, César, 1892-1938.
   [Heraldos negros. English]
   The black heralds / César Vallejo; translated by Kathleen Ross and Richard Schaaf.
      p.   cm. -- (Discoveries)
   Translation of: Los heraldos negros.
   ISBN 0-935480-43-9
   1. Vallejo, César, 1892-1938--Translations, English.
I. Title. II. Series.
PQ8497.V35H413   1990
861--dc20   89-13959
                                          CIP

This project is supported in part by a grant from the National Endowment for the Arts in Washington, D.C., a federal agency.

Originally published as *Los heraldos negros*, Lima, Peru, 1918

Cover: woodcut by Dea Trier Mørch

The Black Heralds may be ordered directly from the publisher:

Latin American Literary Review Press
2300 Palmer Street, Pittsburgh, PA 15218
Tel (412) 351-1477 Fax (412) 351-6831

ACKNOWLEDGMENT

We wish to extend our deepest thanks to another translator and lover of Vallejo: Hardie St. Martin. Hardie's incisive, fresh suggestions and critical comments on many of these poems helped us immeasurably to render this book into English.

TABLE OF CONTENTS

César Vallejo: A Chronology................................13

Los heraldos negros..............................16
The Black Heralds 17

Plafones ágiles
Agile Soffits

Deshojación sagrada............................20
Sacred Falling of Leaves.......................21

Comunión......................................22
Communion.....................................23

Nervazón de angustia 24
Fit of Anguish 25

Bordas de hielo...............................26
Icy Gunwhales 27

Nochebuena....................................28
Christmas Eve 29

Ascuas..30
Burning Coals 31

Medialuz......................................32
Twilight......................................33

Sauce...34
Willow 35

Ausente.......................................36
Away..37

Avestruz......................................38
Ostrich.......................................39

Bajo los álamos...............................40
Under the Poplars.............................41

Buzos
Divers

La araña 44
The Spider 45

Babel...46
Babel...47

Romería 48
Pilgrimage 49

El palco estrecho...50
The Narrow Theater Box 51

De la tierra
Of the Earth

¿···.................54
············?..55

El poeta a su amada.......................................56
The Poet to His Beloved 57

Verano..58
Summer..59

Setiembre...60
September 61

Heces...62
Dregs...63

Impía...64
Godless Woman...65

La copa negra...66
The Black Cup 67

Deshora...68
Unseasonable Time 69

Fresco..70
Fresco..71

Yeso..72
Gypsum..73

Nostalgias imperiales
Imperial Nostalgias

Nostalgias imperiales I..76
Imperial Nostalgias I...77
II..78
III...80
IV 82

Hojas de ébano...84
Leaves of Ebony 85

Terceto Autóctono I..88
Autochthonous Tercet I...89
II..90
III...92

Oración del camino...94
Oration of the Road..95

Huaco..96
Huaco..97

Mayo...98
May..99

Aldeana...102
Village Scene 103

Idilio muerto 104
Dead Idyll 105

Truenos
Thunderclaps

En las tiendas griegas...108
In the Greek Tents..109

Agape 110
Agape 111

La voz del espejo....................................112
The Voice in the Mirror.............................113

Rosa Blanca...114
White Rose..115

La de a mil...116
Win a Thousand......................................117

El pan nuestro......................................118
Our Daily Bread.....................................119

Absoluta..120
Absolute Doctrine...................................121

Desnudo en barro 122
Naked in Clay 123

Capitulación..124
Surrender 125

Líneas 126
Lines 127

Amor prohibido 128
Forbidden Love......................................129

La cena miserable...................................130
The Miserable Supper 131

Para el alma imposible de mi amada..................132
For the Impossible Soul of My Beloved...............133

El tálamo eterno....................................134
The Eternal Marriage Bed 135

Las piedras 136
The Stones 137

Retablo...138
Altarpiece..139

Pagana 140
Pagan Woman 141

Los dados eternos.................................142
The Eternal Dice..................................143

Los anillos fatigados.............................144
The Weary Circles.................................145

Santoral 146
Book of Saints 147

Lluvia..148
Rain..149

Amor 150
Love 151

Dios..152
God...153

Unidad..154
Unity...155

Los arrieros......................................156
The Mule Drivers..................................157

Canciones de hogar
Songs of Home

Encaje de fiebre..................................160
Feverlace...161

Los pasos lejanos.................................162
Distant Footsteps 163

A mi hermano Miguel 164
To My Brother Miguel 165

Enereida..166
January Epic......................................167

Espergesia..170
Last Words..171

Notes on the Translators..........................174

Qui potest capere capiat.

—The Gospel

CESAR VALLEJO: A CHRONOLOGY

1892 - César Vallejo is born in the provincial capital of Santiago de Chuco in northern Perú.

1910 - He enrolls at the university in Trujillo as a student of letters.

1911 - Out of money, Vallejo leaves school and goes to work as a tutor on a hacienda in the mining town of Quiruvilca.

1913 - He returns to the university on his savings and receives his Bachelor's degree two years later. After graduating, Vallejo supports himself teaching grade school.

1918 - Vallejo travels to Lima and meets many intellectuals, including Abraham Valdelomar, who agrees to write the prologue to his first book. Vallejo's first book of poetry, *Los heraldos negros* [*The Black Heralds*], appears.

1920 - Vallejo returns home after two years away. He becomes entangled in a violent town feud in which a deputy is killed and a store is razed. Vallejo is blamed as an accomplice in the incident and later found guilty as the intellectual instigator. He spends 105 days in jail in Trujillo. In jail, he writes some of the poems published in *Trilce*, his second book of poetry, and the story "Fabla salvaje" ["Savage Fable"]. He is cleared and released largely because of the protests of Perú's artistic and intellectual community.

1922 - Vallejo's second book of poetry, *Trilce,* is published.

1923 - Vallejo leaves Perú for Paris, never to return. From 1923 to 1924, Vallejo lives a poverty-stricken bohemian life in Paris, moving from hotel to hotel and associating with many artists and writers residing on Paris' left bank.

1925 - Vallejo secures his first stable job with Le Bureau des Grands Journaux Ibero-americains. He receives a writing grant from the Peruvian Embassy in Madrid and travels to Spain for the first time.

1926 - With Juan Larrea, he co-edits the magazine *Favorables París Poema*, which publishes Huidobro, Neruda, Reverdy, Tzara and Gris. He becomes a columnist for *Variedades*, published in Lima, and writes two important essays: "Poesía Nueva" ["New Poetry"] and "Contra el secreto Profesional" ["Against the Professional Secret"].

1928 - Vallejo throws himself into studying Marxism-Leninism. He makes his first trip to the Soviet Union where he meets and interviews Mayakovsky.

1929 - He marries a French woman, Georgette Philippart. Along with Mariátegui, he breaks with the Peruvian revolutionary movement, APRA, and begins teaching in worker cells. He decides not to write poetry, in the belief that the writer's first role is to be revolutionary. He travels to the Soviet Union for the second time.

1930 - He publishes articles on his trips to Russia in the Madrid magazine *Bolívar*. He travels to Spain for the second time and meets Salinas, Alberti, Unamuno, Lorca and Gerardo Diego. He writes a play entitled *Moscú contra Moscú* [Moscow Against Moscow]. Back in Paris doing political work, the Vallejos are arrested and expelled from France in December. They go to Spain.

1931 - In Madrid he writes the novel *El Tungsteno*, [*Tungsten*] based on his earlier experiences living among the miners in Perú. La Editorial Ulises publishes *Rusia en 1931* [Russia in 1931] a collection of essays based on his trips to Russia. It goes into a second and third edition. He travels to Russia and participates in the International Congress of Authors in Moscow. He returns to Madrid and writes a second book of essays *Rusia ante el Segundo Plan Quinquenal* [Russia Before the Second Five-Year-Plan], another play, *Lockout,* and a children's story "Paco Yunque". Vallejo officially joins the Communist Party.

1932 - The Chautemps government grants the Vallejos permission to return to France. Mme Vallejo returns to Paris to make arrangements and finds their apartment ransacked by the police. Vallejo returns to Paris a month later. Vallejo now collects his articles, notes and diary entries into two books: *Arte y revolución* [*Art and Revolution*] and *Contra el secreto Profesional* [Against the Professional Secret]. He is unable to find a publisher for any of these works, and thus the Vallejos find themselves once again poverty stricken and living at the edge. From 1932 to 1935, Vallejo grows more and more depressed and ill from the strain of having to do odd jobs to barely survive, while at the same time seeking more stable work.

1936 - Vallejo finally finds work teaching Spanish. He publishes *El hombre y Dios en la escultura incaica* [Man and God in Incan Sculpture] in the journal *Beaux-Arts*. The outbreak of Fascism in Spain in July throws Vallejo into political activity. He attends rallies, meetings, raises money and participates in worker cells. He travels to the Spanish front. He returns to Paris in December, completely engaged in the fight against the fascist assault in Spain.

1937 - He founds, with others, the Comité Ibero-americano for the defense of the Spanish Republic, and its propaganda organ, "Nuestra España" [Our Spain]. Vallejo leaves again for Spain to take part in the Second International Writers Congress for the Defense of Culture which meets in Valencia, Madrid and Barcelona, and closes in Paris. The Spanish Civil War ignites Vallejo's poetic sensibility which had been extinguished for over ten years. Back in Paris, he turns all his energy to writing his finest poems that would become his *Poemas Humanos* [*Human Poems*]. He also writes a small collection of poems for the Republican soldiers at the front entitled *España, aparta de mí este Cáliz* [*Spain, Take This Cup from Me*], which is printed by Republican soldiers at the front. During this time when he was writing poetry at a feverish pace, Luis Valcárcel, who saw a good deal of him, says they talked of starting a magazine together in Lima. Vallejo reserves passage for himself and his wife to Perú, but they never leave.

1938 - Vallejo is stricken ill with a high fever and has to be hospitalized. Medical tests are unable to determine the cause of his illness. On April 14th, Vallejo loses consciousness, and on Good Friday, April 15th, César Vallejo dies.

Los heraldos negros

Hay golpes en la vida, tan fuertes... Yo no sé!
Golpes como del odio de Dios; como si ante ellos,
la resaca de todo lo sufrido
se empozara en el alma... Yo no sé!

Son pocos; pero son... Abren zanjas oscuras
en el rostro más fiero y en el lomo más fuerte.
Serán talvez los potros de bárbaros atilas;
o los heraldos negros que nos manda la Muerte.

Son las caídas hondas de los Cristos del alma,
de alguna fe adorable que el Destino blasfema.
Esos golpes sangrientos son las crepitaciones
de algún pan que en la puerta del horno se nos quema.

Y el hombre... Pobre... pobre! Vuelve los ojos, como
cuando por sobre el hombro nos llama una palmada;
vuelve los ojos locos, y todo lo vivido
se empoza, como charco de culpa, en la mirada.

Hay golpes en la vida, tan fuertes... Yo no sé!

The Black Heralds

There are blows in life, so hard... I just don't know!
Blows as from God's hatred; as if, before them,
the backwash of everything suffered
welled-up in the soul... I just don't know!

They are few, but they are... They open dark furrows
in the fiercest face and in the strongest back.
Perhaps they are the steeds of barbarian Attilas,
or the black heralds Death sends us.

They are the deep falls of the Christs of the soul,
of some worshipping faith Destiny blasphemes.
Those bloody blows are the crackling
of some bread burning up on us at the oven door.

And man... Poor... poor man! Turns his eyes, as
when a slap on the shoulder summons us;
turns his eyes wild, and everything lived
wells-up like a pool of guilt in his gaze.

There are blows in life, so hard... I just don't know!

Plafones ágiles

Agile Soffits

Deshojación sagrada

Luna! Corona de una testa inmensa,
que te vas deshojando en sombras gualdas!
Roja corona de un Jesús que piensa
trágicamente dulce de esmeraldas!

Luna! Alocado corazón celeste
¿por qué bogas así, dentro la copa
llena de vino azul, hacia el oeste,
cual derrotada y dolorida popa?

Luna! Y a fuerza de volar en vano,
te holocaustas en ópalos dispersos:
tú eres talvez mi corazón gitano
que vaga en el azul llorando versos!...

Sacred Falling of Leaves

Moon! Crown of an immense head,
you go losing your leaves in golden shadows!
Red crown of a Jesus who thinks
tragically sweet of emeralds!

Moon! Wild, celestial heart,
why are you rowing this way, in the cup
full of blue wine, towards the west,
such a routed and aching stern?

Moon! And by flying off in vain,
you holocaust yourself into scattered opals:
perhaps you are my gypsy heart
that wanders in the blue, wailing poems!...

Comunión

Linda Regia! Tus venas son fermentos
de mi noser antiguo y del champaña
negro de mi vivir!

Tu cabello es la ignota raicilla
del árbol de mi vid.
Tu cabello es la hilacha de una mitra
de ensueño que perdí!

Tu cuerpo es la espumante escaramuza
de un rosado Jordán;
y ondea, como un látigo beatífico
que humillara a la víbora del mal!

Tus brazos dan la sed de lo infinito,
con sus castas hespérides de luz,
cual dos blancos caminos redentores
dos arranques murientes de una cruz.
Y están plasmados en la sangre invicta
de mi imposible azul!

Tus pies son dos heráldicas alondras
que eternamente llegan de mi ayer!
Linda Regia! Tus pies son las dos lágrimas
que al bajar del Espíritu ahogué,
un Domingo de Ramos que entré al Mundo,
ya lejos para siempre de Belén!

Communion

Beautiful Regia! Your veins are the ferments
of my ancient unbeing and the black champagne
of my living!

Your hair is the unknown little root
of the tree of my vine.
Your hair is the loose filament of a mitre
of fantasy I lost!

Your body is the foaming skirmish
of a rose-colored Jordan;
and it undulates, like a beatific whip
that would have humbled the viper of evil!

Your arms make me thirst for the infinite
with their pure Hesperian light,
like two, white, redeeming roads,
two dying uprootings of a cross.
And they are molded in the unconquerable blood
of my impossible blue!

Your feet are two heraldic larks
that eternally arrive from my yesterday!
Beautiful Regia! Your feet are the two tears
I drowned, descending from the Spirit
one Palm Sunday when I entered the World
faraway from Bethlehem forever!

Nervazón de angustia

Dulce hebrea, desclava mi tránsito de arcilla;
desclava mi tensión nerviosa y mi dolor...
Desclava, amada eterna, mi largo afán y los
dos clavos de mis alas y el clavo de mi amor!

Regreso del desierto donde he caído mucho;
retira la cicuta y obséquiame tus vinos:
espanta con un llanto de amor a mis sicarios,
cuyos gestos son férreas cegueras de Longinos!

Desclávame mis clavos ¡oh nueva madre mía!
¡Sinfonía de olivos, escancia tu llorar!
Y has de esperar, sentada junto a mi carne muerta,
cuál cede la amenaza, y la alondra se va!

Pasas... vuelves... Tus lutos trenzan mi gran cilicio
con gotas de curare, filos de humanidad,
la dignidad roquera que hay en tu castidad,
y el judithesco azogue de tu miel interior.

Son las ocho de una mañana en crema brujo...
Hay frío... Un perro pasa royendo el hueso de otro
perro que fue... Y empieza a llorar en mis nervios
un fósforo que en cápsulas de silencio apagué!

Y en mi alma hereje canta su dulce fiesta asiática
un dionisíaco hastío de café...!

Fit of Anguish

Sweet Hebrew woman, unnail my passage of clay;
unnail my nervous strain and my pain...
Unnail, eternal beloved, my long laboring anxiety and
the two nails from my wings and the nail of my love!

I return from the desert where I have fallen many times;
remove the hemlock and serve me your wines:
scare off my paid assassins with a cry of love,
whose wry faces are iron blindnesses of Longinus!

Unnail my nails, oh new mother of mine.
Symphony of olive trees, pour the wine of your weeping!
And you have to wait, seated next to my dead flesh,
while the threat recedes, and the lark takes off!

You go... you return... Your mourning crape braids my great
hair shirt
with drops of curare, sword-edges of humanity,
the rocky dignity that there is in your chastity,
and the Judithesque quicksilver of your inner honey.

It is eight o'clock on a pale, eery morning...
It is cold... A dog goes by gnawing on the bone of another
dog that was... And a match I put out
in capsules of silence begins crying in my veins!

And in my heretic soul a Dionysiac loathing of coffee
sings its sweet Asiatic rejoicing...!

Bordas de hielo

Vengo a verte pasar todos los días,
vaporcito encantado siempre lejos...
Tus ojos son dos rubios capitanes;
tu labio es un brevísimo pañuelo
rojo que ondea en un adiós de sangre!

Vengo a verte pasar; hasta que un día,
embriagada de tiempo y de crueldad,
vaporcito encantado siempre lejos,
la estrella de la tarde partirá!

Las jarcias; vientos que traicionan; vientos
de mujer que pasó!
Tus fríos capitanes darán orden;
y quien habrá partido seré yo...

Icy Gunwhales

I come everyday to watch you pass by,
little enchanted steamer always faraway...
Your eyes are two blond captains;
your lip is a tiny red handkerchief
waving in a goodbye of blood!

I come to watch you pass by; until one day,
drunk on time, on cruelty,
little enchanted steamer always faraway
the evening star will leave!

The shrouds; winds that betray; winds
from a woman who passed by!
Your cold captains will give the order,
and who will have left will be I...!

Nochebuena

Al callar la orquesta, pasean veladas
sombras femeninas bajo los ramajes,
por cuya hojarasca se filtran heladas
quimeras de luna, pálidos celajes.

Hay labios que lloran arias olvidadas,
grandes lirios fingen los ebúrneos trajes.
Charlas y sonrisas en locas bandadas
perfuman de seda los rudos boscajes.

Espero que ría la luz de tu vuelta;
y en la epifanía de tu forma esbelta,
cantará la fiesta en oro mayor.

Balarán mis versos en tu predio entonces,
canturreando en todos sus místicos bronces
que ha nacido el niño-jesús de tu amor.

Christmas Eve

When the orchestra stops playing, hidden
feminine shadows stroll under the branches,
icy chimeras of moonlight, pale swift clouds
filter through the leaves.

There are lips that cry forgotten arias,
ivory gowns feign huge lilies.
Conversation and smiles in wild flocks
perfume the rough forests with silk.

I hope the light of your return will be happy;
and in the Epiphany of your lithe form
the rejoicing will sing in gold Major.

Then my poems will bleat on your fields
humming in all their mystical bronzes
that the Child-Jesus of your love has been born.

Ascuas

Para Domingo Parra del Riego

Luciré para Tilia, en la tragedia
mis estrofas en ópimos racimos;
sangrará cada fruta melodiosa,
como un sol funeral, lúgubres vinos.
Tilia tendrá la cruz
que en la hora final será de luz!

Prenderé para Tilia, en la tragedia,
la gota de fragor que hay en mis labios;
y el labio, al encresparse para el beso,
se partirá en cien pétalos sagrados.
Tilia tendrá el puñal,
el puñal floricida y auroral!

Ya en la sombra, heroína, intacta y mártir,
tendrás bajo tus plantas a la Vida;
mientras veles, rezando mis estrofas,
mi testa, como una hostia en sangre tinta!
Y en un lirio, voraz,
mi sangre, como un virus, beberás!

Burning Coals

for Domingo Parra del Riego

For Tilia, I will hold up my stanzas in the tragedy
in rich, fruitful bunches;
every melodious fruit will bleed,
like a funereal sun, somber wines.
Tilia will hold the cross
that in the final hour will be made of light!

For Tilia, I will ignite in the tragedy the drop
of sound on my lips;
and on curling for the kiss, my lip
will split open into a hundred sacred petals.
Tilia will hold the dagger,
the flower-killing and auroral dagger!

Now in the shadow, heroine, virgin and martyr,
you will have Life at your feet;
while you watch over my head, praying
my stanzas, like a Host in blood-red ink!
And you will drink, ravenous,
my blood like a virus, in a lily!

Medialuz

He soñado una fuga. Y he soñado
tus encajes dispersos en la alcoba.
A lo largo de un muelle, alguna madre;
y sus quince años dando el seno a una hora.

He soñado una fuga. Un "para siempre"
suspirando en la escala de una proa;
he soñado una madre;
unas frescas matitas de verdura,
y el ajuar constelado de una aurora.

A lo largo de un muelle...
Y a lo largo de un cuello que se ahoga!

Twilight

I have dreamed a flight. And I have dreamed
your laces strewn in the bedroom.
Along a pier, some mother;
and her fifteen years breast-feeding an hour.

I have dreamed a flight. A "forever"
whispered on the ramp of a prow.
I have dreamed a mother;
some fresh sprigs of verdure,
and the starry trousseau of an aurora.

Along a pier...
And along a throat that is drowning!

Sauce

Lirismo de invierno, rumor de crespones,
cuando ya se acerca la pronta partida;
agoreras voces de tristes canciones
que en la tarde rezan una despedida.

Visión del entierro de mil ilusiones
en la propia tumba de mortal herida.
Caridad verónica de ignotas regiones,
donde a precio de éter se pierda la vida.

Cerca de la aurora partiré llorando;
y mientras mis años se vayan curvando,
curvará guadañas mi ruta veloz.

Y ante fríos óleos de luna muriente,
con timbres de aceros en tierra indolente,
cavarán los perros, aullando, un adiós!

Willow

Lyricism of winter, murmur of crapes,
when now the early departure nears;
diviner's voices of sad songs
that in the evening pray a farewell.

Vision of the burial of my illusions
in the same tomb as the mortal wound.
Veronica's charity from unknown regions
where, at the price of ether, life is lost.

Near the dawn I will depart, crying;
and while my years go on curving,
my swift route will curve scythes.

And under the cold oils of the dying moon,
with tones of steel in the indolent earth,
the dogs will dig, howling, a goodbye!

Ausente

Ausente! La mañana en que me vaya
más lejos de lo lejos, al Misterio,
como siguiendo inevitable raya,
tus pies resbalarán al cementerio.

Ausente! La mañana en que a la playa
del mar de sombra y del callado imperio,
como un pájaro lúgubre me vaya,
será el blanco panteón tu cautiverio.

Se habrá hecho de noche en tus miradas;
y sufrirás, y tomarás entonces
penitentes blancuras laceradas.

Ausente! Y en tus propios sufrimientos
ha de cruzar entre un llorar de bronces
una jauría de remordimientos!

Away

Away! The morning when I go away
farther than far to the Mystery,
as if following an inevitable ray,
your feet will slip to the cemetery.

Away! The morning when I go away
like a mournful bird to the shore
of the sea of shadow and the silent empire,
the white pantheon will be your captivity.

Night will have fallen in your gaze;
and you will suffer, and then you will grasp
penitent lacerated whitenesses.

Away! And into your own suffering,
amidst a cry of bronzes, will cross
a pack of hounds of remorse!

Avestruz

Melancolía, saca tu dulce pico ya;
no cebes tus ayunos en mis trigos de luz.
Melancolía, basta! Cuál beben tus puñales
la sangre que extrajera mi sanguijuela azul!

No acabes el maná de mujer que ha bajado;
yo quiero que de él nazca mañana alguna cruz,
mañana que no tenga yo a quién volver los ojos,
cuando abra su gran O de burla el ataúd.

Mi corazón es tiesto regado de amargura;
hay otros viejos pájaros que pastan dentro de él...
Melancolía, deja de secarme la vida,
y desnuda tu labio de mujer...!

Ostrich

Melancholy, pull out your gentle beak now;
don't fatten your fast on my wheatfields of light.
Melancholy, enough! How your daggers drink
the blood that my blue leech would draw out!

Don't finish the manna of woman which has fallen;
I want some cross to be born from it tomorrow,
tomorrow when there will be no one to turn my eyes to,
when the coffin opens its great O of mockery.

My heart is an earthen vessel watered with bitterness;
there are other old birds that feed in it...
Melancholy, quit drying up my life,
and reveal your lip of woman...!

Bajo los álamos

Para José Garrido.

Cual hieráticos bardos prisioneros,
los álamos de sangre se han dormido.
Rumian arias de yerba al sol caído,
las greyes de Belén en los oteros.

El anciano pastor, a los postreros
martirios de la luz, estremecido,
en sus pascuales ojos ha cogido
una casta manada de luceros.

Labrado en orfandad baja el instante
con rumores de entierro, al campo orante
y se otoñan de sombra las esquilas.

Supervive el azul urdido en hierro,
y en él, amortajadas las pupilas,
traza su aullido pastoral un perro.

Under the Poplars

for José Garrido

Like imprisoned priestly poets,
the poplars of blood have gone to sleep.
On the hills the flocks of Bethlehem
chew arias of grass as the sun sets.

At the last martyrdoms of light,
the old shepherd, trembling,
has caught a chaste cluster of brilliant
morning stars in his paschal eyes.

Formed in orphanage, now he goes down
with rumors of burial to the praying field;
and the sheepbells are tempered with darkness.

The blue survives warped in iron,
and on it, pupils shrouded,
a dog traces its pastoral howl.

Buzos

Divers

La araña

Es una araña enorme que ya no anda;
una araña incolora, cuyo cuerpo,
una cabeza y un abdomen, sangra.

Hoy la he visto de cerca. Y con qué esfuerzo
hacia todos los flancos
sus pies innumerables alargaba.
Y he pensado en sus ojos invisibles,
los pilotos fatales de la araña.

Es una araña que temblaba fija
en un filo de piedra;
el abdomen a un lado,
y al otro la cabeza.

Con tantos pies la pobre, y aún no puede
resolverse. Y, al verla
atónita en tal trance,
hoy me ha dado qué pena esa viajera.

Es una araña enorme, a quien impide
el abdomen seguir a la cabeza.
Y he pensado en sus ojos
y en sus pies numerosos…
¡Y me ha dado qué pena esa viajera!

The Spider

It's an enormous spider that no longer goes;
a colorless spider, whose body,
a head and an abdomen, is bleeding.

Today I have watched it, up close. And with what effort
towards every flank
it was extending its innumerable feet!
And I've thought about its invisible eyes,
deadly pilots of the spider.

It's a spider that was trembling, stuck
on the edge of a stone;
its abdomen over one side,
its head over the other.

With so many feet, poor thing, and still unable
to resolve itself. And on seeing it aghast
in such a crisis
today I feel so bad for that traveler.

It's an enormous spider, whose abdomen keeps
it from following its head.
And I've thought about its eyes,
its numerous feet...
And I feel so bad for that traveler!

Babel

Dulce hogar sin estilo, fabricado
de un solo golpe y de una sola pieza
de cera tornasol. Y en el hogar
ella daña y arregla; a veces dice:
"El hospicio es bonito; aquí no más!"
¡Y otras veces se pone a llorar!

Babel

Sweet home without style, built
with a single blow and a single piece
of sunflower wax. And in the home
she breaks and fixes; at times says:
"The hospice is nice; I can't take it here!"
Other times she just starts to cry!

Romería

Pasamos juntos. El sueño
lame nuestros pies qué dulce;
y todo se desplaza en pálidas
renunciaciones sin dulce.

Pasamos juntos. Las muertas
almas, las que, cual nosotros,
cruzaron por el amor,
con enfermos pasos ópalos,
salen en sus lutos rígidos
y se ondulan en nosotros.

Amada, vamos al borde
frágil de un montón de tierra.
Va en aceite ungida el ala,
y en pureza. Pero un golpe,
al caer yo no sé dónde,
afila de cada lágrima
un diente hostil.

Y un soldado, un gran soldado,
heridas por charreteras,
se anima en la tarde heroica,
y a sus pies muestra entre risas,
como una gualdrapa horrenda,
el cerebro de la Vida.

Pasamos juntos, muy juntos,
invicta Luz, paso enfermo;
pasamos juntos las lilas
mostazas de un cementerio.

Pilgrimage

We walk together. Sleep
laps our feet, how gently;
and everything is taking place in pale,
how harsh renunciations.

We walk together. The dead
souls, who, like ourselves,
crossed for love
with ailing, opaline footsteps,
come out in their stiff crapes
and wave within in us.

Beloved, we go to the fragile edge
of a mound of earth.
A wing goes by anointed in oil
and in purity. But a blow
falling from I don't know where
sharpens every tear
into a hostile tooth.

And a soldier, a great soldier,
wounds for epaulets,
takes heart in the heroic evening,
and, laughing, shows at his feet,
like a horrendous tattered rag,
the skull of Life.

We walk together, very together,
ailing footsteps, invincible Light,
together we walk by the mustard lilacs
of a cemetery.

El palco estrecho

Más acá, más acá. Yo estoy muy bien.
Llueve; y hace una cruel limitación.
Avanza, avanza el pie.

Hasta qué hora no suben las cortinas
esas manos que fingen un zarzal?
Ves? Los otros, qué cómodos, qué efigies.
Más acá, más acá!

Llueve. Y hoy tarde pasará otra nave
cargada de crespón;
será como un pezón negro y deforme
arrancado a la esfíngica Ilusión.

Más acá, más acá. Tu estás al borde
y la nave arrastrarte puede al mar.
Ah, cortinas inmóviles, simbólicas…
Mi aplauso es un festín de rosas negras:
cederte mi lugar!
Y en el fragor de mi renuncia,
un hilo de infinito sangrará.

Yo no debo estar tan bien;
avanza, avanza el pie!

The Narrow Theater Box

Move closer, closer. I'm just fine.
It's raining; and that is a cruel confinement.
Advance, advance the cue.

How long before those hands like briers
raise the curtain?
See? The others, how comfortable! What effigies!
Move closer, closer!

It's raining. And today will bring another ship
loaded with crape;
it will be like a black, deformed nipple
yanked from the Sphinx-like Illusion.

Move closer, closer! You are on the brink
and the ship may haul you out to sea.
Oh, immobile curtain, symbolic...
My applause is a feast of black roses:
you can have my seat!
And in the thunder of my resignation
a thread of infinity will bleed.

I must not be so fine;
advance, advance the cue!

De la tierra

Of the Earth

54

¿ · · · · · · · · · · · · ·

—Si te amara... qué sería?
—Una orgía!
—Y si él te amara?
Sería
todo rituario, pero menos dulce.

Y si tú me quisieras?
La sombra sufriría
justos fracasos en tus niñas monjas.

Culebrean latigazos,
cuando el can ama a su dueño?
—No; pero la luz es nuestra.
Estás enfermo... Vete... Tengo sueño!

(Bajo la alameda vesperal
se quiebra un fragor de rosa.)
—Idos, pupilas, pronto...
Ya retoña la selva en mi cristal!

. . . . ?

"If I loved you.... what then?"
"An orgy!"
"And if he loved you?"
It would be
all ceremony, but less sweet.

And if you loved me?
The darkness would suffer
a just defeat at the hands of your little nuns.

When the dog loves its master,
does the snaking whip crack?
"No; but the light is ours."
You're sick... Go away... I need to sleep!

(Under the vesperal poplar grove,
a clamor of roses breaks in).
"Go away, orphan girls, hurry..."
Already the jungle is climbing in my window!

El poeta a su amada

Amada, en esta noche tú te has crucificado
sobre los dos maderos curvados de mi beso;
y tu pena me ha dicho que Jesús ha llorado,
y que hay un viernesanto más dulce que ese beso.

En esta noche rara que tanto me has mirado,
la Muerte ha estado alegre y ha cantado en su hueso.
En esta noche de setiembre se ha oficiado
mi segunda caída y el más humano beso.

Amada, moriremos los dos juntos, muy juntos;
se irá secando a pausas nuestra excelsa amargura;
y habrán tocado a sombra nuestros labios difuntos.

Y ya no habrán reproches en tus ojos benditos;
ni volveré a ofenderte. Y en una sepultura
los dos nos dormiremos, como dos hermanitos.

The Poet to His Beloved

Beloved, tonight you have sacrificed yourself
on the two curved timbers of my kiss;
and your grief has told me that Jesus has wept,
and that there's a Good Friday sweeter than that kiss.

On this strange night when you've gazed on me so much,
Death has been happy and has sung in his bones.
On this September night, my second fall
and the most human kiss have been officiated.

Beloved, the two of us will die together, very together;
our sublime bitterness will slowly start drying out;
and our dead lips will have touched in darkness.

And no longer will there be reproaches in your blessed eyes;
nor will I ever again offend you. And in one grave
the two of us will sleep, as little brother and sister.

Verano

Verano, ya me voy. Y me dan pena
las manitas sumisas de tus tardes.
Llegas devotamente; llegas viejo;
y ya no encontrarás en mi alma a nadie.

Verano! Y pasarás por mis balcones
con gran rosario de amatistas y oros,
como un obispo triste que llegara
de lejos a buscar y bendecir
los rotos aros de unos muertos novios.

Verano, ya me voy. Allá, en setiembre
tengo una rosa que te encargo mucho;
la regarás de agua bendita todos
los días de pecado y de sepulcro.

Si a fuerza de llorar el mausoleo,
con luz de fe su mármol aletea,
levanta en alto tu responso, y pide
a Dios que siga para siempre muerta.
Todo ha de ser ya tarde;
y tú no encontrarás en mi alma a nadie.

Ya no llores, Verano! En aquel surco
muere una rosa que renace mucho...

Summer

Summer, I'm leaving now. And the delicate,
submissive hands of your evenings sadden me.
You arrive devoutly; you arrive old;
and now you won't find anyone in my soul.

Summer! And you will walk by my balconies
with a great rosary of amethyst and gold,
like a sad bishop who would come
from faraway to seek and bless
the broken rings of some dead lovers.

Summer, I'm leaving now. Over there, in September
I have a rose that I entrust to you completely;
you will water it with holy water
all the days of sin and tomb.

And if from crying, the mausoleum
flutters its marble wings with the light of faith,
raise on high your response, and pray to
God that the light stay forever dead.
It's all too late now;
and you won't find anyone in my soul.

Don't cry anymore, Summer! In that furrow,
a rose dies that blossoms again and again...

Setiembre

Aquella noche de setiembre, fuiste
tan buena para mí... hasta dolerme!
Yo no sé lo demás; y para eso,
no debiste ser buena, no debiste.

Aquella noche sollozaste al verme
hermético y tirano, enfermo y triste.
Yo no sé lo demás... y para eso,
yo no sé por qué fui triste... tan triste...!

Sólo esa noche de setiembre dulce,
tuve a tus ojos de Magdala, toda
la distancia de Dios... y te fui dulce!

Y también fue una tarde de setiembre
cuando sembré en tus brasas, desde un auto,
los charcos de esta noche de diciembre.

September

That September night, you were
so good to me... so good it even hurt me!
I don't know about the rest; and for that matter
you shouldn't have been so good, you shouldn't have.

That night you sobbed to find me
hermetic and tyrannical, sick and sad.
I don't know about the rest... and for that matter
I don't know why I was sad... so sad...!

That night alone in sweet September
I held your Magdalene eyes, the whole
ranging distance of God... and I was sweet to you!

And also one September evening when,
from a decree, I sowed in your burning coals
the pools of this night in December.

Heces

Esta tarde llueve, como nunca; y no
tengo ganas de vivir, corazón.

Esta tarde es dulce. Por qué no ha de ser?
Viste gracia y pena; viste de mujer.

Esta tarde en Lima llueve. Y yo recuerdo
las cavernas crueles de mi ingratitud;
mi bloque de hielo sobre su amapola,
más fuerte que su "No seas así!"

Mis violentas flores negras; y la bárbara
y enorme pedrada; y el trecho glacial.
Y pondrá el silencio de su dignidad
con óleos quemantes el punto final.

Por eso esta tarde, como nunca, voy
con este búho, con este corazón.

Y otras pasan; y viéndome tan triste,
toman un poquito de ti
en la abrupta arruga de mi hondo dolor.

Esta tarde llueve, llueve mucho. ¡Y no
tengo ganas de vivir, corazón!

Dregs

This evening it's raining more than ever; and I have no
desire to live, heart.

This evening is sweet. Why shouldn't it be?
It's dressed in grace and pain. It's dressed like a woman.

It is raining this evening in Lima. And I remember
the cruel caverns of my ingratitude;
my block of ice over her poppy,
stronger than her "don't be this way!"

My violent black flowers; and the horrible,
barbarous stoning; and the glacial distance.
And with scalding oil the silence of her dignity
will mark the final word.

So this evening, more than ever, I am
with this owl, this heart.

And other women go by; and seeing me so sad
they take on a bit of you
in the craggy wrinkle of my deep sorrow.

It is raining this evening, pouring rain. And I have no
desire to go on living, heart!

Impía

Señor! Estabas tras los cristales
humano y triste de atardecer;
y cuál lloraba tus funerales
    esa mujer!

Sus ojos eran el jueves santo,
dos negros granos de amarga luz!
Con duras gotas de sangre y llanto
    clavó tu cruz!

Impía! Desde que tú partiste
Señor, no ha ido nunca al Jordán,
en rojas aguas su piel desviste,
y al vil judío le vende pan!

Godless Woman

Lord! You were behind the windows,
human and sad as night fell;
and how that woman was crying
           your funeral!

Her eyes were Holy Thursday,
two black grains of bitter light!
With hard drops of blood and a rush of tears
           she nailed your cross!

Godless woman! Ever since you left,
Lord, she never goes down to the Jordan;
in red waters she undresses her flesh,
and she sells bread to the vile Jew!

La copa negra

La noche es una copa de mal. Un silbo agudo
del guardia la atraviesa, cual vibrante alfiler.
Oye, tú, mujerzuela, ¿cómo, si ya te fuiste,
la onda aún es negra y me hace aún arder?

La Tierra tiene bordes de féretro en la sombra.
Oye, tú, mujerzuela, no vayas a volver.

Mi carne nada, nada
en la copa de sombra que me hace aún doler;
mi carne nada en ella,
como en un pantanoso corazón de mujer.

Ascua astral... He sentido
secos roces de arcilla
sobre mi loto diáfano caer.
Ah, mujer! Por ti existe
la carne hecha de instinto. Ah, mujer!

Por eso ¡oh, negro cáliz! aun cuando ya te fuiste,
me ahogo con el polvo,
y piafan en mis carnes más ganas de beber!

The Black Cup

The night is a cup of evil. A shrill police
whistle cuts across it, like a vibrating pin.
Hey you, slut: how come, if you've gone,
the wave is still black and still makes me burn?

The Earth has coffin's edges in the darkness.
Hey you, slut: don't come back.

My flesh swims, swims
in the cup of darkness that still hurts me;
my flesh swims in there,
as in a swampy heart of woman.

Astral red-hot coals... I've felt
dry rubbings of clay fall
over my diaphanous lotus.
Ah, woman! The flesh
of instinct exists because of you. Ah woman!

That's why—oh, black cup!—even now when you've gone
I'm choking on the dust;
and more desires to drink paw in my flesh!

Deshora

Pureza amada, que mis ojos nunca
llegaron a gozar. Pureza absurda!

Yo sé que estabas en la carne un día,
cuando yo hilaba aún mi embrión de vida.

Pureza en falda neutra de colegio;
y leche azul dentro del trigo tierno

a la tarde de lluvia, cuando el alma
ha roto su puñal en retirada,

cuando ha cuajado en no sé qué probeta
sin contenido una insolente piedra,

cuando hay gente contenta; y cuando lloran
párpados ciegos en purpúreas bordas.

Oh, pureza que nunca ni un recado
me dejaste, al partir del triste barro

ni una migaja de tu voz; ni un nervio
de tu convite heroico de luceros.

Alejaos de mí, buenas maldades,
dulces bocas picantes...

Yo la recuerdo al veros ¡oh, mujeres!
Pues de la vida en la perenne tarde,
nació muy poco ¡pero mucho muere!

Unseasonable Time

Beloved purity, that my eyes never
came to enjoy. Absurd purity!

I know you were in the flesh one day
when I was still spinning my embryo of life.

Purity in a school girl's neuter skirt;
and blue milk in the tender wheat

on a rainy afternoon, when the soul
has shattered its retreating dagger,

when an insolent stone has coagulated
in who knows what empty test tube,

when there are happy people; and when
blinded eyelids cry in purple rims.

Oh, purity that never left me even
one message, on leaving the sad clay

not one crumb of your voice; not one nerve
of your heroic feast of morning stars.

Get away from me, good evils,
sweet hot mouths...

I remember it when I see you—oh women!
Because from life in the perennial evening
so little was born, but much is dying!

Fresco

Llegué a confundirme con ella,
tanto...! Por sus recodos
espirituales, yo me iba
jugando entre tiernos fresales,
entre sus griegas manos matinales.

Ella me acomodaba después los lazos negros
y bohemios de la corbata. Y yo
volvía a ver la piedra
absorta, desairados los bancos, y el reloj
que nos iba envolviendo en su carrete,
al dar su inacabable molinete.

Buenas noches aquellas,
que hoy la dan por reír
de mi extraño morir,
de mi modo de andar meditabundo.
Alfeñiques de oro,
joyas de azúcar
que al fin se quiebran en
el mortero de losa de este mundo.

Pero para las lágrimas de amor,
los luceros son lindos pañuelitos
lilas,
naranjos,
verdes,
que empapa el corazón.
Y si hay ya mucha hiel en esas sedas,
hay un cariño que no nace nunca,
que nunca muere,
vuela otro gran pañuelo apocalíptico,
la mano azul, inédita de Dios!

Fresco

I came to confuse myself with her,
so much...! Through her spiritual turns
I was playing among fresh strawberry patches,
among her morning Grecian hands.

Afterwards, she would arrange my black,
bohemian tie. And I
would again see the absorbed
stone, the empty benches, and the clock
that was winding us up on its reel,
to the stroke of its endless circles.

Those were good nights
that today make one laugh
at my strange dying,
my pensive, musing way of going.
Sweet icings of gold,
jewels of sugar
that in the end only break
on the slab mortar of this world.

But for the tears of love
the morning stars are lovely little
lilac,
orange,
green
handkerchiefs the heart soaks through.
And if there is much bitterness now in those silks,
there is a tenderness that is never born,
that never dies,
another great apocalyptic handkerchief flies,
the blue, unedited hand of God!

Yeso

Silencio. Aquí se ha hecho ya de noche,
ya tras del cementerio se fue el sol;
aquí se está llorando a mil pupilas:
no vuelvas; ya murió mi corazón.
Silencio. Aquí ya todo está vestido
de dolor riguroso; y arde apenas,
como un mal kerosone, esta pasión.

Primavera vendrá. Cantarás "Eva"
desde un minuto horizontal, desde un
hornillo en que arderán los nardos de Eros.
¡Forja allí tu perdón para el poeta,
que ha de dolerme aún,
como clavo que cierra un ataúd!

Mas... una noche de lirismo, tu
buen seno, tu mar rojo
se azotará con olas de quince años,
al ver lejos, aviado con recuerdos
mi corsario bajel, mi ingratitud.

Después, tu manzanar, tu labio dándose,
y que se aja por mí por la vez última,
y que muere sangriento de amar mucho,
como un croquis pagano de Jesús.

Amada! Y cantarás;
y ha de vibrar el femenino en mi alma,
como en una enlutada catedral.

Gypsum

Silence. Here, night has fallen already,
already the sun went down behind the cemetery;
here it is crying a thousand pupils:
don't come back; my heart has already died.
Silence. Here, everything is already dressed
in deep mourning; and this passion,
like bad kerosene, barely burns.

Spring will come. You will sing "Eve"
from a horizontal minute, from a
furnace in which the spikenards of Eros burn.
Forge in there your forgiveness for the poet,
that will go on hurting me,
like a nail that shuts a coffin!

But... one night of lyricism, your
good breasts, your red sea
will lash with fifteen-year-old waves,
on seeing in the distance my pirate ship
loaded with memories, my ingratitude.

Afterwards, your apple orchard, your lip giving itself,
that humbles itself for me for the last time,
that dies bloody from so much loving,
like a pagan sketch of Jesus.

Beloved! And you will sing;
and the feminine in my soul will resound
as in a cathedral cloaked in mourning.

Nostalgias imperiales

Imperial Nostalgias

Nostalgias imperiales

I

En los paisajes de Mansiche labra
imperiales nostalgias el crepúsculo;
y lábrase la raza en mi palabra,
como estrella de sangre a flor de músculo.

El campanario dobla... No hay quien abra
la capilla... Diríase un opúsculo
bíblico que muriera en la palabra
de asiática emoción de este crepúsculo.

Un poyo con tres potos, es retablo
en que acaban de alzar labios en coro
la eucaristía de una chicha de oro.

Más allá, de los ranchos surge el viento
el humo oliendo a sueño y a establo,
como si se exhumara un firmamento.

Imperial Nostalgias

I

In the Mansiche landscapes the twilight
shapes imperial nostalgias;
and the race takes shape in my words,
like a star of blood on the surface of muscle.

The belfry tolls... There's no one to open
the chapel... A Biblical booklet
would say that its words died
from this twilight's Asiatic emotion.

A stone bench with three feet is the altarpiece
on which a chorus of lips have just raised
the Eucharist of golden *chicha*.

Beyond, smoke smelling of sleep and barn
rises on the wind from the farms,
as if a firmament had been exhumed.

chicha: beer fermented from maize.

II

La anciana pensativa, cual relieve
de un bloque pre-incaico, hila que hila;
en sus dedos de Mama el huso leve
la lana gris de su vejez trasquila.

Sus ojos de esclerótica de nieve
un ciego sol sin luz guarda y mutila...!
Su boca está en desdén, y en calma aleve
su cansancio imperial talvez vigila.

Hay ficus que meditan, melenudos
trovadores incaicos en derrota,
la rancia pena de esta cruz idiota,

en la hora en rubor que ya se escapa,
y que es lago que suelda espejos rudos
donde náufrago llora Manco-Cápac.

II

Like a relief on a pre-Incan block,
the pensive old woman spins and spins;
in her Mama fingers the light spindle
shears the grey wool of her old age.

A blind sun without light yellows and mutilates
her snowy, sclerotic eyes...!
Her mouth is in disdain, and with deceptive calm
her imperial weariness perhaps keeps vigil.

There are woven hats that meditate, long-haired
defeated Incan troubadours,
the rancid pain of this idiotic cross,

at this blushing hour that now escapes,
that is a lake which solders crude mirrors
where shipwrecked Manco-Capac cries.

Manco-Capac: the first Inca and founder of the Inca Empire.

III

Como viejos curacas van los bueyes
camino de Trujillo, meditando...
Y al hierro de la tarde, fingen reyes
que por muertos dominios van llorando.

En el muro de pie, pienso en las leyes
que la dicha y la angustia van trocando:
ya en las viudas pupilas de los bueyes
se pudren sueños que no tienen cuándo.

La aldea, ante su paso, se reviste
de un rudo gris, en que un mugir de vaca
se aceite en sueño y emoción de huaca.

Y en el festín del cielo azul yodado
gime en el cáliz de la esquila triste
un viejo coraquenque desterrado.

III

Like ancient Indian chiefs, the oxen go
down the road to Trujillo, meditating...
And in the iron of the evening, they feign kings
who go through silent dominions, crying.

Leaning against the wall, I ponder the laws
that happiness and anguish keep on exchanging:
already in the widowed eyes of the oxen
dreams that can never be are rotting.

The village, as they pass, is dressed
in a harsh gray, in which a mooing of cows
is oiled with the dream and emotion of *huaca*.

And in the feast of an iodine-blue sky
an old, outcast *coraquenque* wails
in the cup of the sad cowbell.

huaca: any sacred artifact or place of the Inca, ranging from springs, caves and rocks to temple mounds and ruins. There are thousands of *huacas* throughout the Andes.

coraquenque (curiquingue): a sacred bird of the Inca resembling the vulture.

IV

La Grama mustia, recogida, escueta
ahoga no sé qué protesta ignota:
parece el alma exhausta de un poeta,
arredrada en un gesto de derrota.

La Ramada ha tallado su silueta,
cadavérica jaula, sola y rota,
donde mi enfermo corazón se aquieta
en un tedio estatual de terracota.

Llega el canto sin sal del mar labrado
en su máscara bufa de canalla
que babea y da tumbos de ahorcado!

La niebla hila una venda al cerro lila
que en ensueños miliarios se enmuralla,
como un huaco gigante que vigila.

（1）

IV

The withered, secluded, uninhabited grass
smothers I don't know what unknown protest:
it resembles the exhausted soul of a poet,
withdrawn in a gesture of defeat.

The tree branches have carved their silhouette,
cadaverous cage, alone and broken,
where my sick heart rests
in a statuesque boredom of terra cotta.

The canto arrives without salt from the sea
dressed in its comic mask of a scoundrel
who drools and slumps over as when hanged!

The mist wraps a bandage around the lilac hill,
surrounded by walls of miles and miles of dreams,
like a gigantic *huaco* keeping vigil.

huaco: a sacred figure, vessel or any artifact placed in *huacas*.

Hojas de ébano

Fulge mi cigarrillo;
su luz se limpia en pólvoras de alerta.
Y a su guiño amarillo
entona un pastorcillo
el tamarindo de su sombra muerta.

Ahoga en una enérgica negrura
el caserón entero
la mustia distinción de su blancura.
Pena un frágil aroma de aguacero.

Están todas las puertas muy ancianas,
y se hastía en su habano carcomido
una insomne piedad de mil ojeras.
Yo las dejé lozanas;
y hoy ya las telarañas han zurcido
hasta en el corazón de sus maderas,
coágulos de sombra oliendo a olvido.
La del camino, el día
que me miró llegar, trémula y triste,
mientras que sus dos brazos entreabría
chilló como en un llanto de alegría.
Que en toda fibra existe,
para el ojo que ama, una dormida
novia perla, una lágrima escondida.

Con no sé qué memoria secretea
mi corazón ansioso.
—¿Señora?... —Sí, señor; murió en la aldea;
aún la veo envueltita en su rebozo...

Leaves of Ebony

My cigarette glows;
its light conjures up flashes of gunpowder.
And in time to its yellow wink
a little shepherd begins to sing
of the tamarind tree, his dead shadow.

The big old house,
the faded distinction of its whiteness,
drowns in an energetic blackness.
The fragile aroma of a heavy downpour lingers.

All the doors have become very old,
and the sleepless pity of a thousand dark-circled eyes
is weary in their worm-eaten color of tobacco.
When I left they were young, fresh;
today cobwebs have already spun themselves
right into the heart of their wood,
clots of darkness smelling of neglect.
The day the one facing the street
saw me arrive, it creaked
as if crying for joy, trembling and sad,
while half-opening its two arms.
Because in every fiber there exists,
for the one dearly loved, a sleeping
beloved pearl, a hidden tear.

My anxious heart
whispers with I don't know what remembrance:
"Señora?..." "Yes, Señor; she died in the village;
I can still see her all wrapped in her shawl..."

Y la abuela amargura
de un cantar neurasténico de paria
¡oh, derrotada musa legendaria!
afila sus melódicos raudales
bajo la noche oscura;
como si abajo, abajo,
en la turbia pupila de cascajo
de abierta sepultura,
celebrando perpetuos funerales,
se quebrasen fantásticos puñales.

Llueve... llueve... Sustancia el aguacero,
reduciéndolo a fúnebres olores,
el humor de los viejos alcanfores
que velan *tahuashando* en el sendero
con sus ponchos de hielo y sin sombrero.

And the ancestral bitterness
of a pariah's neurasthenic song
—oh defeated legendary muse!—
sharpens its melodious outpouring
under the darkness of night:
as if below, below,
fantastic daggers were desecrating
the old, muddy eye
of an open grave,
celebrating perpetual funerals.

It is raining.... raining... The downpour condenses,
reduced to funereal odors,
the humor of old camphor trees
awake all night on the path watching over the Empire
in their frozen ponchos and without their hats.

Terceto autóctono

I

El puño labrador se aterciopela,
y en cruz en cada labio se aperfila.
Es fiesta! El ritmo del arado vuela;
y es un chantre de bronce cada esquila.

Afílase lo rudo. Habla escarcela...
En las venas indígenas rutila
un yaraví de sangre que se cuela
en nostalgias de sol por la pupila.

Las pallas, aquenando hondos suspiros,
como en raras estampas seculares,
enrosarian un símbolo en sus giros.

Luce el Apóstol en su trono, luego;
y es, entre inciensos, cirios y cantares,
el moderno dios-sol para el labriego.

Autochthonous Tercet

I

The laboring fist becomes soft as velvet,
and traces a cross on every lip.
It's *fiesta!* The rhythm of the plow takes flight;
and every cowbell is a bronze precentor.

The rough is honed. The hunter's pouch talks....
In indigenous veins shines
a *yaraví* of blood, filtered
through pupils into nostalgias of sun.

The *pallas*, letting out deep sighs like *quenas,*
as in rare, centuries-old prints,
string a rosary of symbols with their twists and turns.

The Apostle appears on his throne, then;
and he is—amidst incense, tall candles and chanting—
a modern sun-god for the peasant.

fiesta: a festive time; joyous party. Many *fiestas* originally were ancient Indian celebrations which were incorporated into Catholic feast days, particularly saints' days.

yaraví: a beautiful, solemn, haunting Quechua song of the Incas. It is often accompanied by the *quena*.

pallas: noblewomen or princesses; wives of the Incas. At *fiesta* time, the women who dance at the head and rear of the street processions are called *pallas*.

quena: a notched flute played by the Indians throughout the Andes.

II

Echa una cana al aire el indio triste.
Hacia el altar fulgente va el gentío.
El ojo del crepúsculo desiste
de ver quemado vivo el caserío.

La pastora de lana y llanque viste,
con pliegues de candor en su atavío;
y en su humildad de lana heroica y triste,
copo es su blanco corazón bravío.

Entre músicas, fuegos de bengala,
solfea un acordeón! Algún tendero
da su reclame al viento: "Nadie iguala!"

Las chispas al flotar lindas, graciosas,
son trigos de oro audaz que el chacarero
siembra en los cielos y en las nebulosas.

II

The sad Indian is having the time of his life.
The crowd heads toward the resplendent altar.
The twilight's eye desists
from watching the little town burned alive.

The shepherdess wears wool and rough sandals,
with pleats of innocence her adornment;
and in her humbleness of sad and heroic wool,
her wild, white heart is a bundle ripe for spinning.

Amidst the music, fireworks,
an accordion sings out! Some shopkeeper
declares to the wind: "No one can match that!"

The lovely, graceful floating sparks
are brazen wheatfields of gold that the farmer
sows in the heavens and in the nebulas.

III

Madrugada. La chicha al fin revienta
en sollozos, lujurias, pugilatos;
entre olores de úrea y de pimienta
traza un ebrio al andar mil garabatos.

"Mañana que me vaya..." se lamenta
un Romeo rural cantando a ratos.
Caldo madrugador hay ya de venta;
y brinca un ruido aperital de platos.

Van tres mujeres... silba un golfo... Lejos
el río anda borracho y canta y llora
prehistorias de agua, tiempos viejos.

Y al sonar una *caja* de Tayanga,
como iniciando un *huaino* azul, remanga
sus pantorrillas de azafrán la Aurora.

III

Daybreak. The *chicha* finally explodes
into sobs, lust, fist fights;
walking amidst odors of urine and pepper,
a drunk traces a thousand winding steps.

A rural Romeo, singing now and then,
laments, "Tomorrow when I go away..."
Now there's early-riser broth for sale;
and an appetizing sound of clinking dishes.

Three women go by... a rake whistles... Far off
the river runs drunk and sings and cries
prehistories of water, old times.

And when a *caja* from Tayanga sounds,
as if initiating a blue *huaino*, the Dawn
unfurls its saffron-colored calves.

caja: a small drum of the Bolivian and Peruvian highlands.

huaino: a traditional costume Indian dance of the Andean highlands in
which couples or a group of people hold hands and dance in circles to
songs sung in Quechua.

Oración del camino

Ni sé para quién es esta amargura!
Oh, Sol, llévala tú que estás muriendo,
y cuelga, como un Cristo ensangrentado,
mi bohemio dolor sobre su pecho.
El valle es de oro amargo;
y el viaje es triste, es largo.

Oyes? Regaña una guitarra. Calla!
Es tu raza, la pobre viejecita
que al saber que eres huésped y que te odian,
se hinca la faz con una roncha lila.
El valle es de oro amargo,
y el trago es largo... largo...

Azulea el camino; ladra el río...
Baja esa frente sudorosa y fría,
fiera y deforme. Cae el pomo roto
de una espada humanicida!

Y en el mómico valle de oro santo,
la brasa de sudor se apaga en llanto!

Queda un olor de tiempo abonado de versos,
para brotes de mármoles consagrados que hereden
la aurífera canción
de la alondra que se pudre en mi corazón!

Oration of the Road

I don't even know who this bitterness is for!
Oh, Sun, you who are dying, take it away
and hang my bohemian pain on their breast
like a bloody Crucifix.
 The valley is full of bitter gold;
 and the journey is sad and long.

Do you hear it? A guitar moaning. Quiet!
It is your race, the poor old woman
who, learning that you are a guest and that they hate you,
bows her face with a purple welt.
 The valley is full of bitter gold,
 and the drink is long... long...

The road is blue; the river barks...
That sweaty and cold, fierce and deformed
head is bowed. The broken pommel
of a humanicidal sword falls!

And in the mummified valley of sacred gold,
hot coals of sweat are put out with a rush of tears!

The fragrance of time lingers, enriched with poems
for the outcrops of consecrated marble that would inherit
the gold-bearing song
of the lark that rots in my heart!

Huaco

Yo soy el coraquenque ciego
que mira por la lente de una llaga,
y que atado está al Globo,
como a un huaco estupendo que girara.

Yo soy el llama, a quien tan sólo alcanza
la necedad hostil a trasquilar
volutas de clarín,
volutas de clarín brillantes de asco
y bronceadas de un viejo yaraví.

Soy el pichón de cóndor desplumado
por latino arcabuz;
y a flor de humanidad floto en los Andes
como un perenne Lázaro de luz.

Yo soy la gracia incaica que se roe
en áureos coricanchas bautizados
de fosfatos de error y de cicuta.
A veces en mis piedras se encabritan
los nervios rotos de un extinto puma.

Un fermento de Sol;
¡levadura de sombra y corazón!

Huaco

I am the blind *coraquenque*
who peers through the lens of a wound,
and who is tied to the Globe,
like a stupendous spinning *huaco*.

I am the llama, whose hostile stupidity
is only reached when sheared by
resounding clarions,
resounding clarions brilliant with disgust
and bronzed with an old *yaraví*.

I am the fledgling condor deplumed
by a Latin harquebus;
and over humanity I soar through the Andes
like an everlasting Lazarus of light.

I am the benevolence of the Inca, eaten away
in golden *coricanchas* baptized
with phosphates of mistake and with hemlock.
At times the shattered nerves of a extinct puma
rear up in my stones.

A ferment of Sun;
yeast of darkness and heart!

coricancha: the sacred garden of the Inca, where life-size golden replicas of corn plants, coca bushes, llamas, alpacas and other plants are placed. These images were among the treasures taken from Cuzco by the Spanish and melted down into gold ingots.

Mayo

Vierte el humo doméstico en la aurora
su sabor a rastrojo;
y canta, haciendo leña, la pastora
un salvaje aleluya!
                    Sepia y rojo.
Humo de la cocina, aperitivo
de gesta en este bravo amanecer.
El último lucero fugitivo
lo bebe, y, ebrio ya de su dulzor,
¡oh celeste zagal trasnochador!
se duerme entre un jirón de rosicler.

Hay ciertas ganas lindas de almorzar,
y beber del arroyo, y chivatear!
Aletear con el humo allá, en la altura;
o entregarse a los vientos otoñales
en pos de alguna Ruth sagrada, pura,
que nos brinde una espiga de ternura
bajo la hebraica unción de los trigales!

Hoz al hombro calmoso,
acre el gesto brioso,
va un joven labrador a Irichugo.
Y en cada brazo que parece yugo
se encrespa el férreo jugo palpitante
que en creador esfuerzo cuotidiano
chispea, como trágico diamante,
a través de los poros de la mano
que no ha bizantinado aún el guante.
Bajo un arco que forma verde aliso,
¡oh cruzada fecunda del andrajo!
pasa el perfil macizo
de este Aquiles incaico del trabajo.

May

Household smoke pours out its savor of left-overs
into the aurora;
and the shepherdess, gathering kindling, sings
a wild hallelujah!
                    Sepia and red.
Smoke from the kitchen, an aperitif
of heroic deeds on this courageous break of day.
The last fugitive evening star
drinks it, and, now drunk on its sweetness,
—Oh celestial, all-night shepherd!—
falls asleep in the turning of a rose-colored dawn.

There are certain beautiful desires to eat lunch,
and drink from the stream, and shout out loud!
To soar high up there, with the smoke;
or to surrender oneself to the autumnal winds
in pursuit of some pure, blessed Ruth
who offers us a spike of tenderness
under the Hebraic unction of wheatfields!

With a sickle over his steady shoulder,
bitterness in his high-spirited face,
a young laborer goes to Irichugo.
And in each yoke-like arm,
the iron juice grows agitated and throbs,
and in an everyday creative effort
sparkles, like a tragic diamond,
through the pores of a hand
no glove has ever adorned.
Under an archway formed of green alder trees,
—Oh fertile crossing of a man in rags!—
passes the massive profile
of this Incan Achilles of labor.

La zagala que llora
su yaraví a la aurora,
recoge ¡oh Venus pobre!
frescos leños fragantes
en sus desnudos brazos arrogantes
esculpidos en cobre.
En tanto que un becerro,
perseguido del perro,
por la cuesta bravía
corre, ofrendando al floreciente día
un himno de Virgilio en su cencerro!

Delante de la choza
el indio abuelo fuma;
y el serrano crepúsculo de rosa,
el ara primitiva se sahúma
en el gas del tabaco.
Tal surge de la entraña fabulosa
de epopéyico huaco,
mítico aroma de broncíneos lotos,
el hilo azul de los alientos rotos!

The shepherdess, who cries
her *yaraví* to the dawn,
gathers,—oh poor Venus!—
fresh, fragrant kindling
in her naked and proud arms
sculpted in copper.
While a calf,
pursued by a dog,
runs across the untamed hill
offering up to the flowering day
a Virgilean hymn in its cowbell.

In front of his hut
the Indian grandfather is smoking;
and the rose-colored dawn on the hills,
the primitive altar, is perfumed
with the scent of tobacco.
Thus rises from the fabulous bowels
of an epic *huaco*,
mythical aroma of bronzed lotuses,
the blue thread of broken lives!

Aldeana

Lejana vibración de esquilas mustias
en el aire derrama
la fragancia rural de sus angustias.
En el patio silente
sangra su despedida el sol poniente.
El ámbar otoñal del panorama
toma un frío matiz de gris doliente!

Al portón de la casa
que el tiempo con sus garras torna ojosa,
asoma silenciosa
y al establo cercano luego pasa,
la silueta calmosa
de un buey color de oro,
que añora con sus bíblicas pupilas,
oyendo la oración de las esquilas,
su edad viril de toro!

Al muro de la huerta,
aleteando la pena de su canto,
salta un gallo gentil, y, en triste alerta,
cual dos gotas de llanto,
tiemblan sus ojos en la tarde muerta!

Lánguido se desgarra
en la vetusta aldea
el dulce yaraví de una guitarra,
en cuya eternidad de hondo quebranto
la triste voz de un indio dondonea,
como un viejo esquilón de camposanto.

De codos yo en el muro,
cuando triunfa en el alma el tinte oscuro
y el viento reza en los ramajes yertos
llantos de quenas, tímidos, inciertos,
suspiro una congoja,
al ver que en la penumbra gualda y roja
llora un trágico azul de idilios muertos!

Village Scene

The distant sound of melancholy cowbells
wafts the rural fragrance
of their anguish into the air.
Onto the silent patio
the setting sun bleeds its farewell.
The autumnal amber of the panorama
takes on a cold tint of painful gray!

On the front door of the house
that time with its claws has filled with holes,
the tranquil silhouette
of a gold-colored ox
silently looms
and then passes to the nearby barn;
and hearing the cowbells' prayer,
its Biblical eyes long for
the virile years of a bull!

A graceful rooster jumps up
onto the garden wall,
fluttering the sorrow of its song,
and in sad alarm,
like two teardrops,
its eyes tremble in the dead afternoon!

Through the old village
tears languidly the haunting *yaraví* on a guitar,
in whose eternity of deep affliction
the sad voice of an Indian rings
like an old cemetery bell.

My head buried in my hands at the wall,
as darkness triumphs in the soul
and the wind prays in the motionless branches
timid, uncertain cries of *quenas*,
I sigh in anguish,
seeing how in the golden-red penumbra
a tragic blue of dead idylls weeps!

Idilio muerto

Qué estará haciendo esta hora mi andina y dulce Rita
de junco y capulí;
ahora que me asfixia Bizancio, y que dormita
la sangre, como flojo cognac, dentro de mí.

Dónde estarán sus manos que en actitud contrita
planchaban en las tardes blancuras por venir;
ahora, en esta lluvia que me quita
las ganas de vivir.

Qué será de su falda de franela; de sus
afanes; de su andar;
de su sabor a cañas de mayo del lugar.

Ha de estarse a la puerta mirando algún celaje,
y al fin dirá temblando: "Qué frío hay... Jesús!"
Y llorará en las tejas un pájaro salvaje.

Dead Idyll

What would my sweet Andean Rita of the rushes and wild
fruit
be doing right now;
now when Byzantium suffocates me, and my blood
dozes, like weak cognac, inside me.

Where would her hands, that in the afternoons
contritely ironed whitenesses yet to come,
be now in this rain that washes away
my desire to go on living.

What has become of her flannel skirt; her
toiling; her walk;
her taste of homemade May brandy.

She must be at her door watching some swift-moving clouds,
and finally she'll say, trembling: "It's so cold... Jesus!"
And a wild bird on the roof tiles will cry.

Truenos

Thunderclaps

En las tiendas griegas

Y el Alma se asustó
a las cinco de aquella tarde azul desteñida.
El labio entre los linos la imploró
con pucheros de novio para su prometida.

El Pensamiento, el gran General se ciñó
de una lanza deicida.
El Corazón danzaba; mas, luego sollozó:
¿la bayadera esclava estaba herida?

Nada! Fueron los tigres que la dan por correr
a apostarse en aquel rincón, y tristes ver
los ocasos que llegan desde Atenas.

No habrá remedio para este hospital de nervios,
para el gran campamento irritado de este atardecer!
Y el General escruta volar siniestras penas
allá.....................................
en el desfiladero de mis nervios!

In the Greek Tents

And the Soul was frightened
at five o'clock that faded blue afternoon.
The lip implored it between the linens,
pouting like a lover to his bride.

Thought, the great General, wore
a god-murdering sword.
The Heart was dancing; but, then it sobbed:
was the Oriental slave-dancer wounded?

Not at all! It was just the tigers who sometimes run
to post themselves in that corner, and sadly watch
the sunsets that arrive from Athens.

There will be no cure for this hospital of nerves,
for the great, irritated encampment of this afternoon!
And the General scrutinizes sinister pains swiftly moving
in   there....................................
through the narrow pass of my nerves!

Agape

Hoy no ha venido nadie a preguntar;
ni me han pedido en esta tarde nada.

No he visto ni una flor de cementerio
en tan alegre procesión de luces.
Perdóname, Señor: qué poco he muerto!

En esta tarde todos, todos pasan
sin preguntarme ni pedirme nada.

Y no sé qué se olvidan y se queda
mal en mis manos, como cosa ajena.

He salido a la puerta,
y me dan ganas de gritar a todos:
Si echan de menos algo, aquí se queda!

Porque en todas las tardes de esta vida,
yo no sé con qué puertas dan a un rostro,
y algo ajeno se toma el alma mía.

Hoy no ha venido nadie;
y hoy he muerto qué poco en esta tarde!

Agape

Today no one's come to call;
nor have they asked me for anything this afternoon.

I haven't seen even one cemetery flower
in such a happy procession of lights.
Forgive me, Lord: how little I have died!

This afternoon everybody, everybody passes by
without calling on me or asking me for anything.

And I don't know what it is they forgot and that's here
feeling bad in my hands, like something strange.

I've gone to the door,
and I want to shout out to everybody:
If you're missing something, here it is!

Because every afternoon of this life,
I don't know what doors they slam in my face,
and my soul is seized by something strange.

Today no one's come;
and today how little I have died this afternoon!

La voz del espejo

Así pasa la vida, como raro espejismo.
¡La rosa azul que alumbra y da el ser al cardo!
Junto al dogma del fardo
matador, el sofisma del Bien y la Razón!

Se ha cogido, al acaso, lo que rozó la mano;
los perfumes volaron, y entre ellos se ha sentido
el moho que a mitad de la ruta ha crecido
en el manzano seco de la muerta Ilusión.

Así pasa la vida,
con cánticos aleves de agostada bacante.
Yo voy todo azorado, adelante... adelante,
rezongando mi marcha funeral.

Van al pie de brahacmánicos elefantes reales,
y al sórdido abejeo de un hervor mercurial,
parejas que alzan brindis esculpidos en roca,
y olvidados crepúsculos una cruz en la boca.

Así pasa la vida, vasta orquesta de Esfinges
que arrojaron al Vacío su marcha funeral.

The Voice in the Mirror

So life goes, like a strange mirage.
The blue rose that illuminates and gives life to the thistle!
Together with the dogma of the murderous
burden, the sophism of Good and Reason!

What the hand touched by chance has been grasped;
perfumes wafted, and among them was the odor of
mould that, halfway down the path, has grown
on the withered apple tree of dead Illusion.

So life goes,
with the deceitful canticles of a withered bacchante.
And, all flustered, I go forward... forward,
mumbling my funeral march.

To the beat of Royal Brahman elephants,
and the sordid buzzing of a mercurial fervor
couples go raising toasts sculpted in rock
and forgotten twilights, a cross on their lips.

So life goes, a vast orchestra of Sphinxes
hurling its funeral march into the Void.

Rosa blanca

Me siento bien. Ahora
brilla un estoico hielo
en mí.
Me da risa esta soga
rubí
que rechina en mi cuerpo.

Soga sin fin,
como una
voluta
descendente
de
mal...
soga sanguínea y zurda
formada de
mil dagas en puntal.

Que vaya así, trenzando
sus rollos de crespón;
y que ate el gato trémulo
del Miedo al nido helado,
al último fogón.

Yo ahora estoy sereno,
con luz.
Y maya en mi Pacífico
un náufrago ataúd.

White Rose

I feel fine. A stoic
ice shines in me
now.
This ruby-red
rope that grates inside my body
makes me laugh.

Endless rope
like a
scroll
descending
from
evil...
Bloody and left-handed rope,
formed from
a thousand pointing daggers.

So let it go, braiding
its rolls of mourning crape;
and let it tie the tremulous cat
of Fear to the frozen den,
the final hearth.

Now surrounded by light,
I am serene.
And out on my Pacific
a shipwrecked coffin mews.

La de a mil

El suertero que grita "La de a mil",
contiene no sé qué fondo de Dios.

Pasan todos los labios. El hastío
despunta en una arruga su yanó.
Pasa el suertero que atesora, acaso
nominal, como Dios,
entre panes tantálicos, humana
impotencia de amor.

Yo le miro al andrajo. Y él pudiera
darnos el corazón;
pero la suerte aquella que en sus manos
aporta, pregonando en alta voz,
como un pájaro cruel, irá a parar
adonde no lo sabe ni lo quiere
este bohemio dios.

Y digo en este viernes tibio que anda
a cuestas bajo el sol:
¡por qué se habrá vestido de suertero
la voluntad de Dios!

Win a Thousand

The lottery ticket vendor who shouts, "Win a thousand!"
possesses I don't know what profound gift of God.

Every lip passes by. Disgust
breaks out in a wrinkle its "Not now."
The lottery ticket vendor passes by, embodying, perhaps
nominally, like God,
among little loaves of cornbread,
a human impotence of love.

I watch this rag of a person. And he could
have given us his heart;
but that luck he holds out in his hands,
hawking loudly
like a cruel bird, will end up
where this bohemian god
neither knows nor cares.

And I say, on this warm Friday
carrying the sun on its back:
why ever would God's will dress up
like a lottery ticket vendor!

El pan nuestro

Para Alejandro Gamboa

Se bebe el desayuno... Húmeda tierra
de cementerio huele a sangre amada.
Ciudad de invierno... La mordaz cruzada
de una carreta que arrastrar parece
una emoción de ayuno encadenada!

Se quisiera tocar todas las puertas,
y preguntar por no sé quién; y luego
ver a los pobres, y, llorando quedos,
dar pedacitos de pan fresco a todos.
Y saquear a los ricos sus viñedos
con las dos manos santas
que a un golpe de luz
volaron desclavadas de la Cruz!

Pestaña matinal, no os levantéis!
¡El pan nuestro de cada día dánoslo,
Señor...!

Todos mis huesos son ajenos;
yo talvez los robé!
Yo vine a darme lo que acaso estuvo
asignado para otro;
y pienso que, si no hubiera nacido,
otro pobre tomara este café!
Yo soy un mal ladrón... A dónde iré!

Y en esta hora fría, en que la tierra
trasciende a polvo humano y es tan triste,
quisiera yo tocar todas las puertas,
y suplicar a no sé quién, perdón,
y hacerle pedacitos de pan fresco
aquí, en el horno de mi corazón...!

Our Daily Bread

for Alejandro Gamboa

You drink your breakfast... The damp earth
of a cemetery smells of beloved blood.
The city in winter... The bitter crossing
of a cart that seems to drag along
a feeling of abstinence in chains!

You want to knock on all the doors,
and ask for who knows who; and then
see the poor, and, crying quietly,
give little pieces of fresh bread to everyone.
And to strip the rich of their vineyards
with the two blessed hands
that with a blow of light
flew off unnailed from the Cross!

Morning eyelashes, don't wake up!
Give us our daily bread,
Lord...!

All my bones belong to others;
perhaps I stole them!
I took for my own what was
meant, perhaps, for another;
and I think that, had I not been born,
another poor man would be drinking this coffee!
I am an awful thief... Where will I go!

And at this cold hour when the earth
smells of human dust and is so sad,
I want to knock on all the doors
and beg who knows who to forgive me,
and bake him little pieces of fresh bread
here, in the oven of my heart...!

Absoluta

Color de ropa antigua. Un julio a sombra,
y un agosto recién segado. Y una
mano de agua que injertó en el pino
resinoso de un tedio malas frutas.

Ahora que has anclado, oscura ropa,
tornas rociada de un suntuoso olor
a tiempo, a abreviación... Y he cantado
el proclive festín que se volcó.

Mas ¿no puedes, Señor, contra la muerte,
contra el límite, contra lo que acaba?
Ay! la llaga en color de ropa antigua,
cómo se entreabre y huele a miel quemada!

Oh unidad excelsa! Oh lo que es uno
por todos!
Amor contra el espacio y contra el tiempo!
Un latido único de corazón;
un solo ritmo: Dios!

Y al encogerse de hombros los linderos
en un bronco desdén irreductible,
hay un riego de sierpes
en la doncella plenitud del l.
¡Una arruga, una sombra!

Absolute Doctrine

The color of old clothes. A July in shadows,
and a just-harvested August. And a
coat of rain that grafted rotten fruit
onto the resinous pine of boredom.

Now that you have dropped anchor, dark clothes,
you return dampened with a rich fragrance
of time, of abbreviation... And I have sung
the evil-inclined feast that capsized.

But, can you not prevail, Lord, against death,
against the limit, against that which ends?
Ay! wound the color of old clothes,
how it opens part-way and smells of burnt honey!

Oh sublime unity! Oh, what is one
for all!
Love against space and time!
A single beat of the heart;
a single rhythm: God!

And as the boundaries shrug their shoulders
in harsh irreducible disdain,
a shower of serpents falls
on the virgin plenitude of 1.
A wrinkle, a shadow!

Desnudo en barro

Como horribles batracios a la atmósfera,
suben visajes lúgubres al labio.
Por el Sahara azul de la Substancia
camina un verso gris, un dromedario.

Fosforece un mohín de sueños crueles.
Y el ciego que murió lleno de voces
de nieve. Y madrugar, poeta, nómada,
al crudísimo día de ser hombre.

Las Horas van febriles, y en los ángulos
abortan rubios siglos de ventura.
¡Quién tira tanto el hilo; quién descuelga
sin piedad nuestros nervios,
cordeles ya gastados, a la tumba!

Amor! Y tú también. Pedradas negras
se engendran en tu máscara y la rompen.
¡La tumba es todavía
un sexo de mujer que atrae al hombre!

Naked in Clay

Like horrible amphibians come up for air,
mournful grimaces rise to the lip.
Through the Sahara of the Substance
walks a gray verse, a dromedary.

A twisted face of cruel dreams glows phosphorescent.
And the blind man who died full of voices
of snow. And rise at dawn, poet, nomad,
to the raw, merciless day of being a man.

The Hours go by feverishly, and in the corners
they miscarry blond centuries of happiness.
Who casts out so much line; who pitilessly
descends our nerves,
already frayed cords, to the tomb?

Love! And you, also. Black blows from a stone
are engendered in your mask, and smash it.
The tomb is yet
a woman's sex that attracts man!

Capitulación

Anoche, unos abriles granas capitularon
ante mis mayos desarmados de juventud;
los marfiles histéricos de su beso me hallaron
muerto; y en un suspiro de amor los enjaulé.

Espiga extraña, dócil. Sus ojos me asediaron
una tarde amaranto que dije un canto a sus
cantos; y anoche, en medio de los brindis, me hablaron
las dos lenguas de sus senos abrasadas de sed.

Pobre trigueña aquella; pobres sus armas; pobres
sus velas cremas que iban al tope en las salobres
espumas de un marmuerto. Vencedora y vencida,

se quedó pensativa y ojerosa y granate.
Yo me partí de aurora. Y desde aquel combate,
de noche entran dos sierpes esclavas a mi vida.

Surrender

Last night, some April seeds surrendered
before my unarmed, youthful Mays;
the hysterical ivories of her kiss found me
dead; and in a sigh of love I caged them away.

Strange, docile spike of wheat. Her eyes besieged me
one amaranthine evening when I recited a canto to her
cantos; and last night, amid the toasts, the two tongues
of her breasts spoke to me, burning up with thirst.

Poor and dark was that woman; poor her weapons; poor
her cream-colored sails flying full-mast over the salt
spray of a dead sea. Victorious and vanquished,

she was left pensive, circles under her eyes, a garnet.
I went away at dawn. And ever since that battle,
at night two serpent slaves enter my life.

Líneas

Cada cinta de fuego
que, en busca del Amor,
arrojo y vibra en rosas lamentables,
me da a luz el sepelio de una víspera.
Yo no sé si el redoble en que lo busco,
será jadear de roca,
o perenne nacer de corazón.

Hay tendida hacia el fondo de los seres,
un eje ultranervioso, honda plomada.
¡La hebra del destino!
Amor desviará tal ley de vida,
hacia la voz del Hombre;
y nos dará la libertad suprema
en transubstanciación azul, virtuosa,
contra lo ciego y lo fatal.

¡Que en cada cifra lata,
recluso en albas frágiles,
el Jesús aún mejor de otra gran Yema!

Y después... La otra línea...
Un Bautista que aguaita, aguaita, aguaita...
Y, cabalgando en intangible curva,
un pie bañado en púrpura.

Lines

Each fiery ribbon
I hurl, in search of Love,
and that vibrates on lamentable roses,
gives birth to the burial of my eve.
I don't know if the throbbing in which I seek it,
will be the panting of rock
or the everlasting birth of heart.

In the depths of beings, there lies
an ultranervous axis, a deep plumb line.
The cord of destiny!
Love will deflect such a law of life
towards the voice of Man;
and will give us supreme liberty
in blue transubstantiation, virtuous
against the blind and ill-fated.

May there beat in every cipher,
secluded in fragile dawns,
an even better Jesus of another great Yolk!

And after that... The other line...
A Baptist who watches, watches, watches...
And, riding on an intangible curve,
a foot bathed in purple.

Amor prohibido

Subes centelleante de labios y ojeras!
Por tus venas subo, como un can herido
que busca el refugio de blandas aceras.

Amor, en el mundo tú eres un pecado!
Mi beso es la punta chispeante del cuerno
del diablo; mi beso que es credo sagrado!

Espíritu es el horópter que pasa
        ¡puro en su blasfemia!
¡el corazón que engendra al cerebro!
que pasa hacia el tuyo, por mi barro triste.
        Platónico estambre
que existe en el cáliz donde tu alma existe!

¿Algún penitente silencio siniestro?
¿Tú acaso lo escuchas? Inocente flor!
... Y saber que donde no hay un Padrenuestro,
el Amor es un Cristo pecador!

Forbidden Love

You rise with lips and dark-circled eyes sparkling!
I rise through your veins, like a wounded dog
looking for the refuge of soft, gentle sidewalks.

Love, you are a sin in this world!
My kiss is the sparkling point of the devil's
horns; my kiss that is a sacred creed!

The eyebeam is a spirit that passes
      pure in its blasphemy!
a heart that engenders the brain!
that passes into yours, through my sad clay.
      Platonic stamen
that exists in the chalice where your soul exists!

Some penitent, sinister silence?
Perhaps you can hear it? Innocent flower!
... And to know that where there is no Our Father,
Love is a sinning Christ!

La cena miserable

Hasta cuándo estaremos esperando lo que
no se nos debe... Y en qué recodo estiraremos
nuestra pobre rodilla para siempre! Hasta cuándo
la cruz que nos alienta no detendrá sus remos.

Hasta cuándo la Duda nos brindará blasones
por haber padecido...
                    Ya nos hemos sentado
mucho a la mesa, con la amargura de un niño
que a media noche, llora de hambre, desvelado...

Y cuándo nos veremos con los demás, al borde
de una mañana eterna, desayunados todos.
Hasta cuándo este valle de lágrimas, a donde
yo nunca dije que me trajeran.
                    De codos
todo bañado en llanto, repito cabizbajo
y vencido: hasta cuándo la cena durará.

Hay alguien que ha bebido mucho, y se burla,
y acerca y aleja de nosotros, como negra cuchara
de amarga esencia humana, la tumba...
                    Y menos sabe
ese oscuro hasta cuándo la cena durará!

The Miserable Supper

How long will we have to wait for all that
is owed us... And in what corner will we
forever bend our humble knees! How long
before the cross that drives us stops its oars.

How long will Doubt keep heralding us
for having suffered....
                    Already we have sat
long at the table, with the bitterness of a child
who cries from hunger, wide awake at midnight...

And when will we join all the others, at the edge
of an eternal morning, everyone breakfasted.
How long in this valley of tears, where
I never asked anyone to bring me.
                    Beaten down,
completely bathed in tears, I repeat, head bowed
and defeated: how long will this supper last.

Someone has drunk a lot, and he mocks us,
and draws near and moves away from us, like a black spoonful
of bitter human essence, the tomb....
                    And that dark, strange man
knows even less how long this supper will last!

Para el alma imposible de mi amada

Amada: no has querido plasmarte jamás
como lo ha pensado mi divino amor.
    Quédate en la hostia,
    ciega e impalpable,
    como existe Dios.

Si he cantado mucho, he llorado más
por ti ¡oh mi parábola excelsa de amor!
    Quédate en el seso,
    y en el mito inmenso
    de mi corazón!

Es la fe, la fragua donde yo quemé
el terroso hierro de tanta mujer;
y en un yunque impío te quise pulir.
    Quédate en la eterna
    nebulosa, ahí,
en la multicencia de un dulce noser.

Y si no has querido plasmarte jamás
en mi metafísica emoción de amor,
    deja que me azote,
    como un pecador.

For the Impossible Soul of My Beloved

Beloved: you have never wanted to take the form
my divine love has planned.
                    Stay in the host,
                    blind and impalpable,
                    as God exists there.

If I have sung much, I have cried even more
for you, oh my sublime parabola of love!
                    Stay in the brain
                    and in the immense myth
                    of my heart!

It is faith, the forge where I burned
the earthy iron of so much woman;
and on an ungodly anvil I wanted to refine you.
                    Stay in the eternal
                    nebula, here,
in the multisense of a sweet unbeing.

And if you have never wanted to take the form
of my metaphysical emotion of love,
                    let me whip myself
                    like a sinner.

El tálamo eterno

Sólo al dejar de ser, Amor es fuerte!
Y la tumba será una gran pupila,
en cuyo fondo supervive y llora
la angustia del amor, como en un cáliz
de dulce eternidad y negra aurora.

Y los labios se encrespan para el beso,
como algo lleno que desborda y muere;
y, en conjunción crispante,
cada boca renuncia para la otra
una vida de vida agonizante.

Y cuando pienso así, dulce es la tumba
donde todos al fin se compenetran
en un mismo fragor;
dulce es la sombra, donde todos se unen
en una cita universal de amor.

The Eternal Marriage Bed

Only when it ceases to be, is Love strong!
And the tomb will be a great eye,
in whose depths the anguish of love
survives and cries, as in a chalice
of sweet eternity and black dawn.

And lips curl up for the kiss,
as when something full overflows and dies;
and, in convulsive union,
each mouth renounces for the other
a life of agonizing, dying life.

And when I think this way, sweet is the tomb
where everyone finally interpenetrates
into one same clamor;
sweet is the darkness, where everyone unites
in a universal tryst of love.

Las piedras

    Esta mañana bajé
a las piedras ¡oh las piedras!
Y motivé y troquelé
un pugilato de piedras.

    Madre nuestra, si mis pasos
en el mundo hacen doler,
es que son los fogonazos
de un absurdo amanecer.

    Las piedras no ofenden; nada
codician. Tan sólo piden
amor a todos, y piden
amor aun a la Nada.

    Y si algunas de ellas se
van cabizbajas, o van
avergonzadas, es que
algo de humano harán...

    Mas, no falta quien a alguna
por puro gusto golpee.
Tal, blanca piedra es la luna
que voló de un puntapié...

    Madre nuestra, esta mañana
me he corrido con las hiedras,
al ver la azul caravana
de las piedras,
de las piedras,
de las piedras...

The Stones

This morning I went down
to the stones, oh the stones!
And I caused and cast
a pugilism of stones.

Our mother, if my footsteps
in the world cause pain,
it's that they are the fiery flashes
of an absurd break of day.

The stones do not offend; they
covet nothing. They only ask
love everyone, and they ask
love even Nothingness.

And if some of them go
away crestfallen, or become
ashamed, it's that
they are bound to do something human...

But, there are always those who will hit
someone for the pure pleasure of it.
And so, the moon is a white stone
that flew off with a kick...

Our mother, this morning
I have run off with the ivy,
on seeing the blue caravan
of the stones,
of the stones,
of the stones...

Retablo

Yo digo para mí: por fin escapo al ruido;
nadie me ve que voy a la nave sagrada.
Altas sombras acuden,
y Darío que pasa con su lira enlutada.

Con paso innumerable sale la dulce Musa,
y a ella van mis ojos, cual polluelos al grano.
La acosan tules de éter y azabaches dormidos,
en tanto sueña el mirlo de la vida en su mano.

Dios mío, eres piadoso, porque diste esta nave,
donde hacen estos brujos azules sus oficios.
Darío de las Américas celestes! Tal ellos se parecen
a ti! Y de tus trenzas fabrican sus cilicios.

Como ánimas que buscan entierros de oro absurdo,
aquellos arciprestes vagos del corazón,
se internan, y aparecen... y, hablándonos de lejos,
nos lloran el suicidio monótono de Dios!

Altarpiece

I tell myself: finally I've escaped the noise;
no one sees me on my way to the sacred nave.
Tall shadows are in attendance,
and Darío who passes with his grieving lyre.

With innumerable steps the sweet Muse comes out,
and my eyes go to her, as chicks to grain.
Ethereal tulles and sleeping titmice pursue her,
while the blackbird of life dreams in her hand.

My God, you are merciful, because you granted this nave,
where these blue sorcerers perform their offices.
Darío of the celestial Americas! They are so much
like you! And from your braids they make their hair shirts.

Like souls who seek buried treasures of absurd gold,
those errant archpriests of the heart
penetrate deep, and appear... and, speaking to us from afar,
weep the monotonous suicide of God!

Pagana

Ir muriendo y cantando. Y bautizar la sombra
con sangre babilónica de noble gladiador.
Y rubricar los cuneiformes de la áurea alfombra
con la pluma del ruiseñor y la tinta azul del dolor.

¿La vida? Hembra proteica. Contemplarla asustada
escaparse en sus velos, infiel, falsa Judith;
verla desde la herida, y asirla en la mirada,
incrustando un capricho de cera en un rubí.

Mosto de Babilonia, Holofernes sin tropas,
en el árbol cristiano yo colgué mi nidal;
la viña redentora negó amor a mis copas;
Judith, la vida aleve, sesgó su cuerpo hostial.

Tal un festín pagano. Y amarla hasta en la muerte,
mientras las venas siembran rojas perlas de mal;
y así volverse al polvo, conquistador sin suerte,
dejando miles de ojos de sangre en el puñal.

Pagan Woman

To go along dying and singing. And to baptize the shadows
with the Babylonian blood of a noble gladiator.
And to initial the cuneiforms of a gold carpet
with a nightingale's quill and the blue ink of sorrow.

Life? A protean female. To watch her flee,
frightened, behind her veils, a heathen, false Judith;
to see her from the wound and seize her in my gaze,
engraving a wax design onto a ruby.

New wine of Babylonia, Holofernes without troops,
I made my nest in the Christian tree;
the redemptive vineyard denied love to my cup;
Judith, perfidious life, reclined her sacrificial body.

So was the pagan feast. And to love her even into death,
while my veins sow red pearls of evil;
and so to return to dust, a luckless conqueror,
leaving thousands of drops of blood on the dagger.

Los dados eternos

> Para Manuel González Prada esta emoción
> bravía y selecta, una de las que, con más
> entusiasmo, me ha aplaudido el gran maestro.

Dios mío, estoy llorando el ser que vivo;
me pesa haber tomádote tu pan;
pero este pobre barro pensativo
no es costra fermentada en tu costado:
tú no tienes Marías que se van!

Dios mío, si tú hubieras sido hombre,
hoy supieras ser Dios;
pero tú, que estuviste siempre bien,
no sientes nada de tu creación.
Y el hombre sí te sufre: el Dios es él!

Hoy que en mis ojos brujos hay candelas,
como en un condenado,
Dios mío, prenderás todas tus velas,
y jugaremos con el viejo dado...
Talvez ¡oh jugador! al dar la suerte
del universo todo,
surgirán las ojeras de la Muerte,
como dos ases fúnebres de lodo.

Dios mío, y esta noche sorda, oscura,
ya no podrás jugar, porque la Tierra
es un dado roído y ya redondo
a fuerza de rodar a la aventura,
que no puede parar sino en un hueco,
en el hueco de inmensa sepultura.

The Eternal Dice

For Manuel González Prada,
this wild and select emotion,
one for which the great master
has applauded me most enthusiastically.

My God, I am crying over the life I live;
it grieves me to have taken your bread from you;
but this poor, pensive piece of clay
isn't a scab fermented in your side:
you don't have Marys who leave you!

My God, if you had been a man,
today you would know how to be God;
but you, who were always fine,
don't feel anything of what your creation feels.
And man does suffer for you: he is the one who is God!

Today there is a fire in my demon eyes,
as in those of a condemned man;
My God, you will light all your candles,
and we will play with the old dice...
Perhaps—O gambler!—throwing the luck
of the whole universe,
the dark-circled eyes of Death will come up,
like two funereal aces of mud.

My God, and on this dark, silent night
you can't play any more, for the Earth
is a die already rounded, worn down
from so much rolling by chance,
that can only stop in a hole,
in the hole of an immense grave.

Los anillos fatigados

Hay ganas de volver, de amar, de no ausentarse,
y hay ganas de morir, combatido por dos
aguas encontradas que jamás han de istmarse.

Hay ganas de un gran beso que amortaje a la Vida,
que acaba en el áfrica de una agonía ardiente,
suicida!

Hay ganas de... no tener ganas, Señor;
a ti yo te señalo con el dedo deicida:
hay ganas de no haber tenido corazón.

La primavera vuelve, vuelve y se irá. Y Dios,
curvado en tiempo, se repite, y pasa, pasa
a cuestas con la espina dorsal del Universo.

Cuando las sienes tocan su lúgubre tambor,
cuando me duele el sueño grabado en un puñal,
¡hay ganas de quedarse plantado en este verso!

The Weary Circles

There is a desire to return, to love, not to go away
and there is a desire to die, fought by two
colliding waters that have never found an isthmus.

There is a desire for a great kiss that would shroud Life,
that ends in the Africa of a burning, suicidal
agony!

There is a desire to... have no desires. Lord,
I point my deicidal finger at you:
there is a desire never to have had a heart.

Spring returns, returns and it will leave. And God,
curved in time, repeats himself, and passes, passes
with the backbone of the Universe on his back.

When my temples beat their mournful drum,
when sleep etched on a dagger hurts me,
there is a desire to stay right here in this poem!

Santoral

(Parágrafos.)

Viejo Osiris! Llegué hasta la pared
de enfrente de la vida.

Y me parece que he tenido siempre
a la mano esta pared.

Soy la sombra, el reverso: todo va
bajo mis pasos de columna eterna.

Nada he traído por las trenzas; todo
fácil se vino a mí, como una herencia.

Sardanápalo. Tal, botón eléctrico
de máquinas de sueño fue mi boca.

Así he llegado a la pared de enfrente;
y siempre esta pared tuve a la mano.

Viejo Osiris! Perdónote! Que nada
alcanzó a requerirme, nada, nada...

Book of Saints

(paragraphs.)

Old Osiris! I came as far as the wall
in front of life.

And it seems to me that I always had
this wall within my grasp.

I am the shadow, the reverse: everything goes by
under my eternal column's steps.

I have nothing to show from struggle; everything
came to me easily, like an inheritance.

Sardanapalus. And so, my mouth was
the electric button of dream machines.

Thus I have come as far as the front wall;
and this wall was always within my grasp.

Old Osiris! I forgive you! For nothing
managed to convince me, nothing, nothing...

Lluvia

En Lima... En Lima está lloviendo
el agua sucia de un dolor
qué mortífero. Está lloviendo
de la gotera de tu amor.

No te hagas la que está durmiendo,
recuerda de tu trovador;
que yo ya comprendo... comprendo
la humana ecuación de tu amor.

Truena en la mística dulzaina
la gema tempestuosa y zaina,
la brujería de tu "sí".

Mas, cae, cae el aguacero
al ataúd de mi sendero,
donde me ahueso para ti...

Rain

In Lima... In Lima it is raining
the foul water of such a deadly
pain! It is raining
through the leak of your love.

Don't pretend to be sleeping,
remember your troubadour;
for now I understand... I understand
the human equation of your love.

The tempestuous and treacherous gem,
the sorcery of your "yes,"
thunders in the mystical sweetness.

But it is pouring rain, pouring
on the coffin of my path,
where I long for you...

Amor

Amor, ya no vuelves a mis ojos muertos;
y cuál mi idealista corazón te llora.
Mis cálices todos aguardan abiertos
tus hostias de otoño y vinos de aurora.

Amor, cruz divina, riega mis desiertos
con tu sangre de astros que sueña y que llora.
¡Amor, ya no vuelves a mis ojos muertos
que temen y ansían tu llanto de aurora!

Amor, no te quiero cuando estás distante
rifado en afeites de alegre bacante,
o en frágil y chata facción de mujer.

Amor, ven sin carne, de un icor que asombre;
y que yo, a manera de Dios, sea el hombre
que ama y engendra sin sensual placer!

Love

Love, you come no more to my dead eyes;
and how my idealistic heart weeps for you.
All my chalices openly await
your Hosts of autumn and wines of dawn.

Love, divine cross, water my deserts
with your astral blood that dreams and weeps.
Love, you come no more to my dead eyes
that dread and long for your tears of dawn!

Love, I don't want you when you are distant,
fought over in your guise of a happy bacchante
or the frail, pretty face of a woman.

Love, come without flesh, from ichor that amazes;
so that I, in the manner of God, may be a man
who loves and engenders without sensual pleasure!

Dios

Siento a Dios que camina
tan en mí, con la tarde y con el mar.
Con él nos vamos juntos. Anochece.
Con él anochecemos. Orfandad...

Pero yo siento a Dios. Y hasta parece
que él me dicta no sé qué buen color.
Como un hospitalario, es bueno y triste;
mustia un dulce desdén de enamorado:
debe dolerle mucho el corazón.

Oh, Dios mío, recién a ti me llego,
hoy que amo tanto en esta tarde; hoy
que en la falsa balanza de unos senos,
mido y lloro una frágil Creación.

Y tú, cuál llorarás... tú, enamorado
de tanto enorme seno girador...
Yo te consagro Dios, porque amas tanto;
porque jamás sonríes; porque siempre
debe dolerte mucho el corazón.

God

I feel God who walks
so much in me, with the evening and the sea.
We go away together. Night falls.
We go into the night together, Orphanhood...

But I feel God. And it even seems
he dictates to me I don't know what good color.
Like a caregiver, he is kind and sad;
he languishes with a lover's sweet disdain:
his heart must ache so much.

Oh, my God, I've only just come to you,
today when this evening I love so much; today
when in the false balance of someone's breasts,
I weigh and weep for a fragile Creation.

And you, which one do you weep for.... You, in love
with such an enormous, spinning breast...
I consecrate you, God, because you love so much;
because you never smile; because always
your heart must ache so much.

Unidad

En esta noche mi reloj jadea
junto a la sien oscurecida, como
manzana de revólver que voltea
bajo el gatillo sin hallar el plomo.

La luna blanca, inmóvil, lagrimea,
y es un ojo que apunta... Y siento cómo
se acuña el gran Misterio en una idea
hostil y ovóidea, en un bermejo plomo.

¡Ah, mano que limita, que amenaza
tras de todas las puertas, y que alienta
en todos los relojes, cede y pasa!

Sobre la araña gris de tu armazón,
otra gran Mano hecha de luz sustenta
un plomo en forma azul de corazón.

Unity

Tonight my clock gasps for breath
next to my darkened temple, like
the chamber of a revolver that turns
past the trigger without finding the bullet.

The white, immobile moon sheds tears,
and is an eye that aims... And I sense how
the great Mystery is coined into a hostile
and ovoid idea, into a bright red bullet.

Ah, hand that limits, that threatens
behind every door, and that breathes
in every clock, give up and leave!

Over the gray spider of your skeletal frame,
another great Hand, made of light, holds
a bullet in the blue shape of a heart.

Los arrieros

Arriero, vas fabulosamente vidriado de sudor.
La hacienda Menocucho
cobra mil sinsabores diarios por la vida.
Las doce. Vamos a la cintura del día.
El sol que duele mucho.

Arriero, con tu poncho colorado te alejas,
saboreando el romance peruano de tu coca.
Y yo desde una hamaca,
desde un siglo de duda,
cavilo tu horizonte, y atisbo, lamentado
por zancudos y por el estribillo gentil
y enfermo de una "paca-paca".
Al fin tú llegarás donde debes llegar,
arriero, que, detrás de tu burro santurrón,
te vas...
te vas...

Feliz de ti, en este calor en que se encabritan
todas las ansias y todos los motivos;
cuando el espíritu que anima al cuerpo apenas,
va sin coca, y no atina a cabestrar
su bruto hacia los Andes
oxidentales de la Eternidad.

The Mule Drivers

Mule driver, you go fabulously glazed in sweat.
The Menocucho hacienda
charges a thousand trials a day to live.
It's twelve noon. We've arrived at the waist of the day.
The sun that hurts so much.

Mule driver, you go off in your red poncho,
savoring the Peruvian romance of your coca.
And I, from a hammock,
from a century of doubt,
ponder your horizon and watch, tormented
by the mosquitoes and by the charming, feeble
refrain of a *paca-paca* bird.
Finally you will end up where you ought to end up,
mule driver, you who, behind your sanctimonious mule,
go away...
go away...

Lucky you, in this heat in which all motives
and all anxieties rear up;
when the spirit that barely enlivens the body
goes without coca, and doesn't even think to lead
its brute towards the western
Andes of Eternity.

Canciones de hogar

Songs of Home

Encaje de fiebre

Por los cuadros de santos en el muro colgados
mis pupilas arrastran un ¡ay! de anochecer;
y en un temblor de fiebre, con los brazos cruzados,
mi ser recibe vaga visita del Noser.

Una mosca llorona en los muebles cansados
yo no sé qué leyenda fatal quiere verter:
una ilusión de Orientes que fugan asaltados;
un nido azul de alondras que mueren al nacer.

En un sillón antiguo sentado está mi padre.
Como una Dolorosa, entra y sale mi madre.
Y al verlos siento un algo que no quiere partir.

Porque antes de la oblea que es hostia hecha de Ciencia,
está la hostia, oblea hecha de Providencia.
Y la visita nace, me ayuda a bien vivir...

Feverlace

Along the paintings of saints on the wall
my pupils drag an ay! of nightfall;
and in a trembling fever, my arms crossed,
my being receives a vague visit from the Unbeing.

A crying fly on the tired furniture
wants to pour out I don't know what fatal legend:
an illusion of Orients that flee, assaulted;
a blue nest of larks that die at birth.

My father sits in an old armchair.
Like a Sorrowing Mary, my mother comes and goes.
And, seeing them, I feel a something that won't go away.

Because before the wafer, host made of Knowledge,
is the Host, wafer made of Providence.
And the visit begins, it helps me to live right...

Los pasos lejanos

Mi padre duerme. Su semblante augusto
figura un apacible corazón;
está ahora tan dulce...
si hay algo en él de amargo, seré yo.

Hay soledad en el hogar; se reza;
y no hay noticias de los hijos hoy.
Mi padre se despierta, ausculta
la huida a Egipto, el restañante adiós.
Está ahora tan cerca;
si hay algo en él de lejos, seré yo.

Y mi madre pasea allá en los huertos,
saboreando un sabor ya sin sabor.
Está ahora tan suave,
tan ala, tan salida, tan amor.

Hay soledad en el hogar sin bulla,
sin noticias, sin verde, sin niñez.
Y si hay algo quebrado en esta tarde,
y que baja y que cruje,
son dos viejos caminos blancos, curvos.
Por ellos va mi corazón a pie.

The Distant Footsteps

My father is asleep. His august countenance
suggests a peaceful heart;
now he is so gentle...
if there's any bitterness in him, it must be me.

There's loneliness in the home; there is praying;
and there's no news of the children today.
My father awakens, hearing inside himself
the Flight into Egypt, the goodbye which stanches the bleeding.
Now he is so near;
if there's any distance in him, it must be me.

And my mother walks out there in the orchard,
savoring a savor now without savor.
Now she is so soft,
so much wing, so much outgoing, so much love.

There's loneliness in the home with no bustling,
no news, no green, no childhood.
And if there's something broken this afternoon,
and that weakens and that creaks,
it is two, old, white curving roads.
Down them my heart goes on foot.

A mi hermano Miguel

In memoriam.

Hermano, hoy estoy en el poyo de la casa,
donde nos haces una falta sin fondo!
Me acuerdo que jugábamos esta hora, y que mamá
nos acariciaba: "Pero, hijos..."

Ahora yo me escondo;
como antes, todas estas oraciones
vespertinas, y espero que tú no des conmigo.
Por la sala, el zaguán, los corredores.
Después, te ocultas tú, y yo no doy contigo.
Me acuerdo que nos hacíamos llorar,
hermano, en aquel juego.

Miguel, tú te escondiste
una noche de agosto, al alborear;
pero, en vez de ocultarte riendo, estabas triste.
Y tu gemelo corazón de esas tardes
extintas se ha aburrido de no encontrarte. Y ya
cae sombra en el alma.

Oye, hermano, no tardes
en salir. Bueno? Puede inquietarse mamá.

To My Brother Miguel

in memoriam.

   Brother, today I'm sitting on the bench outside our house.
Where you are missed so deeply!
I remember how we used to play at this hour, and that mama
would hug and caress us: "But, boys..."

   Now I hide,
just like before, all those evening
prayers, and I hope you can't find me.
Through the living room, the entryway, the halls.
Then, you hide, and I can't find you.
I remember we made each other cry,
brother, in that game.

   Miguel, you hid
one night in August, just before dawn;
but, instead of hiding laughing, you were sad.
And your twin heart of those extinct evenings
has gotten tired of not finding you. And now
shadow falls across the soul.

   Hey, brother, don't take so long
coming out. Okay? Mama might get worried.

Enereida

Mi padre, apenas,
en la mañana pajarina, pone
sus setentiocho años, sus setentiocho
ramos de invierno a solear.
El cementerio de Santiago, untado
en alegre año nuevo, está a la vista.
Cuántas veces sus pasos cortaron hacia él,
y tornaron de algún entierro humilde.

Hoy hace mucho tiempo que mi padre no sale!
Una broma de niños se desbanda.

Otras veces le hablaba a mi madre
de impresiones urbanas, de política;
y hoy, apoyado en su bastón ilustre
que sonara mejor en los años de la Gobernación,
mi padre está desconocido, frágil,
mi padre es una víspera.
Lleva, trae, abstraído, reliquias, cosas,
recuerdos, sugerencias.
La mañana apacible le acompaña
con sus alas blancas de hermana de caridad.

Día eterno es éste, día ingenuo, infante,
coral, oracional;
se corona el tiempo de palomas,
y el futuro se puebla
de caravanas de inmortales rosas.
Padre, aún sigue todo despertando;
es enero que canta, es tu amor
que resonando va en la Eternidad.
Aún reirás de tus pequeñuelos,
y habrá bulla triunfal en los Vacíos.

January Epic

My father, barely,
in the bird-filled morning, puts
his seventy-eight years, his seventy-eight
boughs of winter out to sun.
The Santiago cemetery, draped
in happy New Year, is in view.
How many times his footsteps have cut over towards it,
and returned from some humble burial.

It's been a long time since my father went out!
A noisy gathering of children breaks up.

Other times he used to talk to my mother
of city matters, politics;
and today, supported by his distinguished cane
that sounded better in his years in the Government,
my father is unrecognizable, fragile,
my father is an eve full of expectation.
He carries, brings, abstracted, relics, things,
memories, suggestions.
The calm morning accompanies him
with its white wings of a sister of charity.

This is an eternal day, a naive day, a child,
a choir boy, prayerful;
time is crowned with doves,
and the future fills
with caravans of immortal roses.
Father, everything is still waking up;
it is January that sings, it is your love
that goes resounding in Eternity.
You will still laugh with your little ones,
and there will be a triumphant uproar in the Void.

Aún será año nuevo. Habrá empanadas;
y yo tendré hambre, cuando toque a misa
en el beato campanario
el buen ciego mélico con quien
departieron mis sílabas escolares y frescas,
mi inocencia rotunda.
Y cuando la mañana llena de gracia,
desde sus senos de tiempo
que son dos renuncias, dos avances de amor
que se tienden y ruegan infinito, eterna vida,
cante, y eche a volar Verbos plurales,
jirones de tu ser,
a la borda de sus alas blancas
de hermana de caridad ¡oh, padre mío!

It will still be New Year's. There will be *empanadas*;
and I will be hungry when Mass is rung
in the blessed belfry
by the lyrical blind man with whom
my fresh and schoolish syllables, my plump innocence,
conversed.
And when the morning full of grace,
from its breasts of time,
that are two renunciations, two advances of love
that lie down and plead for infinity, eternal life,
sings, and lets fly more words than the Word,
torn pieces of your being,
on the fringe of its white wings
of a sister of charity, oh, my father!

Espergesia

Yo nací un día
que Dios estuvo enfermo.

Todos saben que vivo,
que soy malo; y no saben
del deciembre de ese enero.
Pues yo nací un día
que Dios estuvo enfermo.

Hay un vacío
en mi aire metafísico
que nadie ha de palpar:
el claustro de un silencio
que habló a flor de fuego.
Yo nací un día
que Dios estuvo enfermo.

Hermano, escucha, escucha...
Bueno. Y que no me vaya
sin llevar diciembres,
sin dejar eneros.
Pues yo nací un día
que Dios estuvo enfermo.

Todos saben que vivo,
que mastico... Y no saben
por qué en mi verso chirrían,
oscuro sinsabor de féretro,
luyidos vientos
desenroscados de la Esfinge
preguntona del Desierto.

Last Words

I was born on a day
God was sick.

Everyone knows that I live,
that I'm bad, and they don't know
about the December of that January.
For I was born on a day
God was sick.

There's an emptiness
in my metaphysical air
that no one's going to touch:
the cloister of a silence
that spoke with its tongue on fire.
I was born on a day
God was sick.

Brother, listen, listen...
Okay now. And don't let me go away
without taking along Decembers,
without leaving Januaries.
For I was born on a day
God was sick.

Everyone knows that I live,
that I chew... And they don't know
why in my poems,
a dark disgust of coffin,
rasp frayed winds
unraveled from the Sphinx,
the great questioner of the Desert.

Todos saben... Y no saben
que la Luz es tísica,
y la Sombra gorda...
Y no saben que el Misterio sintetiza...
que él es la joroba
musical y triste que a distancia denuncia
el paso meridiano de las lindes a las Lindes.

Yo nací un día
que Dios estuvo enfermo,
grave.

Everyone knows... And they don't know
that the Light is consumptive,
and the Shadow fat...
And they don't know the Mystery sums it up...
that it is the hump
musical and sad that in the distance denounces
the meridian passage from the limits to the Limits.

I was born on a day
God was sick,
grave.

ABOUT THE TRANSLATORS

RICHARD SCHAAF has translated two books of essays by César Vallejo: *The Mayakovsky Case* and *Autopsy on Surrealism* (Curbstone Press, 1983). He has edited and translated the selected poetry of the Salvadoran poet Roque Dalton, as well as co-translating his long collage-poem *A Red Book for Lenin* and his testimonial novel, *Miguel Mármol*. He has also co-translated the complete writings of the Nicaraguan poet Leonel Rugama. His last translation effort is a book of essays by the Bolivian filmmaker Jorge Sanjinés, *Theory and Practice of a Cinema With the People*. He lives in Washington, D.C.

KATHLEEN ROSS teaches Spanish American literature at Duke University. She is the translator of works by Nicolás Guillén and Alejo Carpentier, and is the co-translator, with Richard Schaaf, of *Miguel Mármol* by Roque Dalton (Curbstone Press, 1987). She has also published several essays of literary criticism.

082023